Love Lies

by Marcia Shein

DORRANCE
PUBLISHING CO
EST. 1920
PITTSBURGH, PENNSYLVANIA 15238

Dorrance Publishing Co
585 Alpha Drive
Pittsburgh, PA 15238
Visit our website at *www.dorrancebookstore.com*

ISBN: 978-1-4809-8884-2
eISBN: 978-1-4809-8838-5

Love Lies

Marisa stood on the roof of what was just another New York building adding its pretentious posture to an already overcrowded view of nothing important. Even though she was in Brooklyn, she could see where the Trade Towers once stood and where now the new single trade tower building ripped through the skyline. The Towers were once the main focus of the New York skyline. Even after they built the memorial and new building, the space once occupied by the Towers would always evoke feelings of sorrow and emptiness, no different than how Marisa felt now.

From where she stood Marisa could smell the fuel-filled air far below from the never-ending city traffic. The only stars were those that managed to be brighter than the lights of the city; the North Star and the moon were all that shined through. She wanted to feel something good about her life again. It was a Friday night and instead of being with her family, particularly her boyfriend and brother, all she could do was hope Saturday would bring some cloud cover as night fell.

For the past twelve months Marisa was confined to the building where she stood with its stale air, overcrowded conditions, and lack of any natural sunlight. She welcomed the daily hour of fresh air she was given, but that too was usually in a caged area. If all went well, Marisa hoped this would be her last two nights in federal prison.

• • •

Kellie Harper was staring out the window of the twenty-second floor where she worked in downtown Atlanta going over what the next few days would bring. Having spent a long week with the corporate suits she worked for, she looked forward to the weekend before she had to leave for Colombia, South America. Sitting there she wondered what had motivated her to leave her previous job of nine years, to become a security consultant to a large corporation involved in developing factory labor for other companies in underutilized third world locations. She did not want to believe she did it for the money, but in reality she knew that was one of the reasons. The high six figures she was offered was hard to turn down from a government salary, even if it was the FBI.

Though she traveled less in this job, her most recent assignment was to travel to an isolated remote area in Colombia and investigate possible factory location sites. Such ventures were cost effective for a company seeking cheaper labor than could be found in the United States. To Kellie it seemed like exploitation of the locals, selling them short on income for low cost goods to be sent to the United States, more exploitation than exploration. With a deep sigh she turned to the phone to call her partner Jan. Jan's ever-vigilant assistant and friend answered the phone.

"Good morning, law office of Jan Bergin and associates. This is David; how can I help you?"

"Hi David, it's Kellie."

"Hi Kellie, everything okay with you?"

"Yes, all is well. Can I speak to Jan if she is not too busy?"

"Well, busy is relative but I know she will want to speak with you, hang on." David transferred the call.

"Hi babe, ," Jan said with enthusiasm, "glad you called. I just got out of court. How are you?"

"Doing ok, just continuing the fight with myself on why I ended up in Corporate America and not law enforcement. How are you doing?"

"I have been working on a case where I think I can save my client at least 10 years if he cooperates. They have so much on him, informants, video surveillance, the usual. Don't sound so sad baby, it's Friday. I know you are still in the early phases of transition to corporate life but you will be amazing at your job with your experience."

"Not sad," Kellie answered, "just not sure about corporate life. There are some new suits in town wanting me to investigate the possibility of setting up a textile factory in some remote parts of Colombia. I will likely have to leave town Sunday to get to this location by Monday and will be gone for at least a week. How about a quiet dinner at home tonight with no cell phones, e-mail, and no TV!"

"Sounds perfect, I will go over my schedule with David, but I should be home around six and yes, date night it is!"

"I love David; he is so good for you."

"That is an understatement; he is the only man I know that can type more than eighty words a minute, answer the phone and keep me organized all at the same time, day after day, and still remain calm. He is the yin to my yang or I am his? Not sure how that goes," Jan said with a laugh. "See you tonight, babe."

"I love you, Kellie."

"I love you too. Talk to you later."

• • •

Jan Bergin sat at her desk looking out the window of her Midtown law office. She had just put aside the court case she mentioned to Kellie. The deal looked done and she wanted to turn her attention to another pressing matter. Jan picked up the Marisa Herrera-Cardosas file to either prepare to resolve her case or start preparing for trial. She did not want to work over the weekend with Kellie leaving on Sunday for Colombia.

"David, can you come in my office for a minute and let me talk to you about Marisa's case?"

"Ok," he replied, walking into her office, "I know this helps you but I won't have any advice, it seems as if there is no way out."

"I know, but I need another ear and it helps to discuss out loud what is going on. I am hoping for inspiration."

Jan began by complaining that the federal government was unwilling to reduce a possible life in prison sentence to anything reasonable for Marisa. She was exposed to a life in prison based on the drug quantities involved in the conspiracy of at least three hundred kilograms of cocaine and well over ten thousand kilograms of marijuana. That was all the government knew about, but the numbers were much bigger based on the entire conspiracy and international players. If, however, she cooperated and testified against the leaders of the organization, the government agreed to inform the judge about her cooperation and request a substantially mitigated sentence, something around ten to fifteen years.

"She has been reluctant to cooperate because it would involve informing on her brother and her lover." Jan revealed to David. "The organization she worked for is big and bad, operating from Colombia through the U.S. Virgin Islands, involving Customs and DEA agents on the take from both countries. They want Marisa to serve a life sentence for her involvement in the organization and will not agree to reduce their recommendation if she continues to refuse to first cooperate fully and then agree to turn in her brother and the man they believe is the U.S. connection and mastermind."

"Well," David contemplated, "why not give the brother and lover up? Maybe you can get a deal for the brother if they both come clean. I know this would be hard for her but what are her options other than life in prison?"

"The Government thinks Marisa can also tell them about the main Colombian connections where the drugs are coming from. Truthfully, she does know all this but has told me she fears that the Cartel connections and even her lover would kill her and her brother if she was known to be cooperating. The Feds need Marisa to fill in the details and identify the agents on the take. The brother is needed to corroborate her story."

"This sounds complicated," David offered. "If Marisa is not interested in telling on her own brother and lover she is destined for something unpleasant to say the least."

"Exactly, and I have been trying to get her to see the big picture if she does not come clean. When Marisa got arrested she got caught in a typical good cop/bad cop trap. She was arrested by the DEA task force out of New York. The agents who picked her up let her cooperate, giving her the impression that she did not have to give up her brother, so she disclosed information about an off-load incident as if this was her main and only involvement in any drug conspiracy. Later the agents said the Assistant United States Attorney assigned to her case also wanted the brother and that she knew more than she was telling the agents. The agents of course backtracked on their original promise and told her she lied and was not forthcoming on important details.

Unfortunately, they were right; Marisa lied about her brother's involvement. What Marisa also failed to tell the agents was that David Stone, the leader of U.S. drug importation business for a Colombian drug family, was also Damian Garrison, her lover."

"She really made a mess of her case. Were you her attorney then?" David asked.

"No she did most of the talking without getting an attorney and before she was assigned a public defender who would have told her to keep her mouth shut. When I got into the case all this had already happened. Based on my advice she is not talking now and won't until she wants to and then and only then telling the whole truth for a good deal, a quid pro quo."

"Jan you are such a fighter for your clients. Too bad she did not have you in her case sooner. This does not look good for Marisa. What's next for her?" asked David.

"Marisa will have to decide if she wants to cooperate against her lover, then convince her brother to cooperate and hope we can get a deal for the brother and her she can live with. I don't know what she wants to do about this David Stone guy or whatever his name is."

"I thought you can't represent both Marisa and the brother. Isn't that a conflict of interest?" David was concerned that Jan could not negotiate a sentence for the brother while representing Marisa without them waiving any conflict, as this is a serious issue in the legal community and bar ethics rules.

"I know, that is a problem, but if I can discuss these options with the Assistant United States Attorney to see where he is coming from I would at least know that it is possible to resolve both cases amicably and then find an attorney for the brother."

"You have your work cut out for you. I can look up this Stone/Garrison guy on Google and see if anything comes up. I could also do some sentencing comparison research on similar cases with and without cooperation."

"That would be great, David. At least I will feel we are doing something productive. Thanks for listening. I appreciate you so much."

"Anytime," David said as he walked out of Jan's office with a smile. We have two families he mused, the one we are born with and the ones we chose to be close to in life's long journey. Jan and Kellie were his chosen family. He would do anything for them in or outside of work but he knew Jan the best and knew how dedicated she was to her work. She never gave up on someone if they showed even a small sign of a willingness to do the right thing in getting their life back. He wanted to help in any way he could.

Jan sat at her desk frustrated as usual at the government not wanting to do a deal that is fair and reasonable.. How could anyone subject a second family member to what Marisa was facing? They both are facing life in prison. What incentive was there for Marisa to cooperate? "I have to find a way," Jan said out loud to no one in particular.

"David, what's next on my schedule?" Jan yelled into the other office.

"I am preparing a motion to continue the Colbert case. I need to finish that first. You can start working on Marisa's pretrial motions as they are due next week if there is no plea agreement."

"Ok," she called back, "I guess for now I have no choice as the case looks like it is going to trial."

Jan thought to herself that she knew Marisa could also disclose how the drugs came through customs in St. Thomas in the Virgin Islands. She told Jan that shipping vessels took the drugs to prearranged ocean drop off points up different parts of the east coast, particularly northern Florida and New York. The captains of these vessels made extra money to throw the containers overboard on their way to ports of call to deliver container goods from around the world. Racing style boats would find the drugs in floating containers with GPS tracking devices attached, pick them up about five miles off shore and bring them to off-load locations. It was a sophisticated operation with a lot of money and muscle. Over seventy percent of the drugs were typically recovered, making the industry a good bet. Marisa had been to the area where the main cartel family lived and worked, so Marisa could expose all of this based on her relationship with Damian Garrison. Marisa disclosed the network information to Jan. To get any help in her case, Marisa would need to disclose this information to the government, something Marisa was not willing to do for now. She either took the risk against grave potential danger as an informant or she and her brother go to jail for life, not much of a choice.

Jan continued to struggle with the information she knew Marisa could offer and how to use that to her advantage. Marisa only got caught because the government indicted several of her co-conspirators, off-loaders and boat drivers, who were caught in the New York harbor. The harbor patrol stopped the boats after they retrieved the cocaine and were headed back to shore because they were running without lights. All four occupants on the boat started talking before they were even booked. One of the off-loaders identified Marisa as a leader and organizer of off-load crews. The Vasquez drug operation delivered drugs up and down the east coast from Florida to New York.

Jan thought about calling the Assistant United States Attorney, Jake Harden one more time. At first he would not help Marisa without DEA and Customs on board and agreeing to a deal. The agents made it clear that they wanted to squeeze Marisa for the brother and then the two of them give up Damian Garrison, only known to the government by the alias David Stone. Without room for compromise, Marisa Herrera-Cardosas was destined to remain in jail for the rest of her life. At 26, that was a long time.

"David, can you get Assistant United States Attorney Jake Harden on the phone?" Jan yelled.

"I thought you were going to work on Marisa's pretrial motions?" David replied with frustration in his voice.

"I am but I want to talk to Harden again about a better deal. Maybe if I bitch and moan enough he will listen and consider a different offer"

"Good luck with that!" David hollered back.

"Just get him on the phone!"

"My fingers are dialing now."

•　　•　　•

Marisa went back to her cubicle, an eight by eight-foot room that was more like a big box than a place for two people to live. The space was taken up with one set of metal bunk beds with a three inch mattress, a metal desk with an attached metal stool and two small upright lockers for legal materials and commissary. Bathrooms were communal with no doors just partitions between the toilets and showers located at the end of two rows of seven cement cubes. There was no privacy anywhere as guards and other inmates were always around.

"I cannot stand this place," Marisa said to Andrea Barrett one of the guards standing nearby.

"What was that you said, Marisa?"

Marisa had made friends with some of the guards. Some were nice and would talk to you like a human being, while others liked the power. Andrea was friendly and Marisa even got her to talk about her problems when time allowed.

"The space in here is claustrophobic. The slightest noise bounces off of the bare concrete block walls and linoleum floor. I can't think clearly. I can't relax!"

"Well Marisa," Andrea mused, "I come in this hellhole every day. I have to check on 28 inmates four times a day during my shift to be sure everyone is accounted for and has not escaped. The pay is pathetic, so we are both in jail. I just get to do it in eight hour shifts." With that Andrea moved on down the row of cubicles, her discontent with all things government apparent on her face.

There was no relief from the continuous coughing, sneezing, and yelling. Marisa tried to block out the sights and sounds that invaded her senses. Alone again with her thoughts, she realized love had taken her to places she was not supposed to go. Marisa let her thoughts drift back to where she started before getting into this mess, trying to quiet her mind from the invasive conditions of prison life.

Like so many small towns in Puerto Rico, the town of Caguas ran with a slow pulse. Most in the community barely made a living and were either in jobs that did not pay well, on welfare, or some other government assistance. It was in her home town that she first met Damian Garrison three years before her arrest. All of this happened before the devastation of Puerto Rico from Hurricane Maria. Now she had no home to even go back to if she ever did get out of prison. All she had was time to think about her life and how she ended up in prison.

Marisa remembered her childhood when things were simple. She never had a lot of toys, but filled her days with make-believe games played in her mind with imaginary friends. She had two dolls, one headless from the local dump and one from a thrift store, neither of which had any clothes and the one with a head had hair that was matted. These dolls were her best friends. She could tell them anything and many days she would spend playing with them as princesses being carried off by a real man, not just a man in a shiny knight's suit on a white horse from the fairy tales.

Marisa had trouble connecting with her parents. They could not see her for who she was, someone who wanted to be loved and protected. Her parents never gave her that support like they did for William. When her little brother, William, was born, she knew he would be the center of her parents' attention. Her parents wanted him to become a politician so they named him William Charles Herrera-Cardosas. Their parents felt that if part of his name was formal sounding, he would command respect. That he did, but not the way his parents hoped.

At a slender, six foot two inches tall, with a deep Puerto Rican tan, dark brown hair and brown eyes, he was known by all the local girls who wanted to date him. He was the tallest boy in the neighborhood so he often stood out in a crowd with his features and personality. He spoke of getting out of Puerto Rico and to have adventures he read about in old *National Geographic* magazines he found at the local dump. He read about exotic places in the world he longed for, but knew he would never be able to visit. He was nothing but a dreamer while Marisa was the star of her high school soccer team made up of mostly boys. She was a straight A student and never missed school, even when she was sick. William, on the other hand, hardly attended school. He spent his time rummaging through garbage dumps or abandoned fields where residents left their household items, from sinks and toilets to paint and batteries. He experimented with chemicals he found. He mixed things up just to see how they smelled or if they would burn. He once blew up an old car on the street by mixing some turpentine with some kind of household cleaner. The smoke from the car fire could be seen for miles. No one knew for sure who had blown up the car except Marisa. When William told her about it, he laughed.

"Marisa," he said pointing in the direction of the smoke, "don't look too hard, but you see all that smoke?"

Marisa did not respond as she knew that he was telling her it was his doing. The local police were suspicious but no one saw William do it. He could build anything out of junk. Once he built an engine from scavenged parts he collected in junkyards over two years. Then he found an old Piper Cub airplane propeller and fashioned an air propelled go-cart. Everyone was impressed until he crashed into the neighbor's dog and it died.

Her parents, when they found out about something William did, either laughed at his antics or paid someone to make his troubles go away, even though they did not have any money to spare. Marisa reminded herself, that despite his antics, she would do the same thing for him. She never wanted anything bad to happen to William. She was the big sister, they were best friends, and he made her laugh at life's challenges with his "I don't care what other people think" attitude.

Despite her frustrations with him she could not help but try and protect him, even now. She wondered if it was all worth it to protect him and Damian. Her love for them both, though different, is what keeps her strong and will save her, she thought. Marisa smiled hoping these memories would not be lost in time.

•   •   •

Damian was getting restless waiting for Marisa to arrive. He hated waiting for anyone in the prison visiting room. While sitting in the waiting room he saw someone that looked familiar. He did not want to be noticed and used his alias David Reisen to come into the prison with a false driver's license in that name for identification purposes.

"Hey David Stone, it's Charlie. Do you remember me? I used to work with you on the docks in St. Thomas."

"Uh, okay." Damian was unsure of who this person was, but he seemed familiar. This guy also used the alias he only used for drug business which made the encounter even more uncomfortable.

"Yeah, you gotta remember, we worked on putting some containers with GPS tracking devices on them on a ship you wanted sent to New York about a year ago. That was a great idea in case someone stole your containers. I was a dockhand and you were there to oversee the shipment. I remember you because you paid me a good cash tip when we were done."

"Oh sure, Charlie, sorry I forgot your last name. What are you doing here?" Damian hoped no one could hear them or realize he was using another false identification to get into the prison.

"A friend got in trouble for being on a boat bringing in some cocaine in the New York harbor."

"Who is it?" asked Damian casually not wanting to sound too interested in knowing who it was.

"His name is Jorge Valero. Do you know him?"

"Uh, no, the name is not familiar." Damian lied. This is one of the fools that got caught and is likely cooperating with the government. He never met Valero, but knew who he was from Marisa who supervised a lot of his off-load crews, of which Valero was a repeat helper.

"Nice to see you, Charlie," Damian said without emotion as he walked to another spot in the visiting room. He did not want to engage in further conversation with this guy out of fear of causing the guards in the visiting room to become suspicious. He hoped this guy did not know what those containers had in them, he wanted nothing more than to get his visit with Marisa over with. In the meantime he let his thoughts drift to his other problems which all seemed to be stacking up.

Damian had to fly into Medellin, Colombia, to see Santos, the right-hand man to Carlos Vasquez Jr., the heir to the drug family he worked for before coming to see Marisa. He recalled flying into the Medellin airport, three days before coming to New York for what he hoped was the last time. It was time to get Marisa ready to execute her part of their plan but the Vasquez family came first.

Damian was worried, he was sorry for the mess he made in a recent Florida off-load but it was necessary. Damian explained to Santos that one of the off-loaders was using, and skimming off of the last cocaine shipment Marisa was working. It was Damien's policy that if you worked for him you do not use the product or steal.

"Damian," Santos said, "Carlos Jr. is not happy about your issues. He sent me to talk to you and bring you in if necessary to talk to his father."

"No need, Santos." Damian advised, "I have it under control."

"Damian, you know we prefer low profile deliveries and conduct," Santos told him. "Now we have two problems, one with the helper you killed and now Marisa's arrest."

For Damian this conversation was just noise. He replied to Santos trying to divert his attention to the reason for his successes not failures. "Yes of course but sometimes you have to take someone out so the others will fear doing the same thing. I know how to handle Marisa's situation. I have a plan."

Santos went on with his concerns to Damian's discontent. "Damian, Junior's father is not going to be happy if he finds out about this mess. You need authorization to kill someone, as it brings to much attention to our operation if not done right. What did you do with the body?"

Damian gave a slight smile over his clever handling of the thieving off-loader and how he led the conversation with Santos in the direction he wanted it to go. Damian thought to himself, *tell them something, just not the whole truth.*

"I disposed of the body using cement shoes," Damian said with a laugh. "He is now about two hundred feet down and six miles off the coast of Florida feeding the fish on the reef." He did not, however, disclose all he knew about Marisa and her cooperation.

As he sat in the prison visiting room, Damian reminded himself that he was not afraid of Santos or the family. He knew too much and had too many hideouts the Vasquez family did not know about. But he also knew the family was not happy with him and the present situation with Marisa's arrest. He had to deal with that as well, but how to do it was something he was still contemplating and had no intentions of telling Santos or anyone else.

"Look Santos," he said during their meeting, "tell the family anything you want, but you know my skills have helped this family for the past five years create a multimillion dollar operation. I have made a business out of an otherwise common drug trafficking ring and outsmarted the law for years. You have to trust me with these problems as well."

Damian was deep in thought amused by his own accomplishments and how easy it was to manipulate Santos and the family selling them his theories of how things should be reminded Santos that his operations were the best in the business and that he made him and the family a lot of money. Santos only response was "remember where you started and who pays the bills". With that Damian thought "yeah, I do."

He alone was the one to set up a network of people that insulated the family and himself, and they knew he improved their profits with his business structure, something the Vasquez family was without before he came along. He met Santos at a bar one night on South Beach. They hit it off and after several drinks, both were discussing how to make money without a regular job. It was Santos who told Damian about the business. Damian was ready to get out of corporate America after working in logistics for a major trucking company in New York. He attended one of the best business schools in the country and wanted to do something more with the skills he learned. The logistics training made him a perfect match for the Vasquez family.

Santos worked with Damian first, to see if he was as good as he bragged. It did not take long for Santos to realize he was a perfect match to the family drug business and conveyed this to patriarch, Carlos Vasquez Sr. Damian knew his plan was perfect. No matter how many people or boats he used, seldom did one group even know the other existed. He would often have two off-loads going on at the same time so that if one was detected, the other would cover costs and losses.

Damian reminded himself that he was paid well for his services, but his ultimate goal was to run the whole show and have his own business and suppliers. The key to his success was never letting anyone know everything about his business or who he really was, including Santos or the Vasquez family. The problem he now faced was that he broke his own rule with Marisa. Despite all of his success he still did not see Marisa's arrest coming. She knew too much, and that was never good for business.

• • •

Marisa was still in her room even though she was expecting Damian to visit her today for a final discussion about their plans for the future. Marisa needed to get out of this hellhole. Time moved slowly in prison, there was nothing to do. On each floor there were no real windows, only an unbreakable, six inch wide, three inch thick slat of glass to view the world outside. Being in a ten story high-rise prison kept you from seeing anything but a sliver of sky. Finally, her name was called and as Marisa walked to the elevator for her visit with Damian she looked out the small window and saw that it was raining.

Though it was Friday, Saturday could not come fast enough. Marisa hoped the rain would come and go, leaving only clouds with little wind. She needed dark cloudy conditions, a little luck, and hope that William and Damian had been able to do what Damian promised on his many visits in the past two months. Their plan was pure genius and she knew that if anyone could pull it off, William and Damian could. She did not see a choice other than to leave the United States on the run from the law until she could find a way out of this mess. She knew Damian had put a master plan in place because he loved her and wanted to be with her for the rest of their lives. That was all she needed.

Marisa's thoughts were interrupted when the elevator stopped on the visiting floor. The prison visiting room was as bare as the unit floors that housed the inmates, cement floors and cinder block walls. Two metal folding chairs faced each other on either side of a matching table. Cameras and guards were ever watchful. Though touching was not allowed, when the visiting room got more crowded Marisa and Damian leaned forward and held hands while they talked. She found Damian in deep thought as she approached and touched his shoulder.

"Damian, are you all right?" she asked.

Startled from his thoughts he replied "Sorry my love, I was in deep thought about our future. I'm here to finalize our plans. Just checking again, you haven't told the feds anything about me, have you?" Damian asked. He was waiting for her to lie as his own sources told him she had done so.

"No, of course not, Damian, I'm in love with you and want us to be together. I would never give you or William up. I just want to get out of here. I would do anything to protect you and my brother. Just like I told you before I have told them only about the off-load event that got me arrested and nothing more. I did not give them the details of what happened or who was behind it all. Of course, they don't believe me but that is all I have said to them."

"Are you sure there is nothing else you want to tell me?" Damian asked knowing there was more.

Marisa admitted some of what she told the agents when she was arrested.

"I told the government some information about a guy named David Stone who would contact me when a shipment was coming but that was related to the off-load that got me arrested. They wanted to know who told me to be somewhere at a particular location and time for the off-loads. I had to tell them something."

Damian was not happy about this. "What were you thinking giving them my alias? Why did you keep this from me? You first told me you gave them nothing other than the information on the off-load where you were arrested."

"I thought it would help since it was not your real name. I thought the government would believe me even though I was lying about a lot of the information I gave them and they would consider a deal that would let me get out sooner than later without exposing you and William. This all happened before you and William got a plan together to get me out of here."

Marisa worried she was telling Damian too much.

"I did not do anything to lead the government to you, I swear I would never give you up. I actually gave them misinformation. I never told them about your tattoos and I gave them a different description of you physically. I told them you were five foot nine inches and a little overweight."

Marisa thought to herself that she also did not give information that Damian had a gunshot wound in his left shoulder from an altercation with a rival drug dealer she never told the government about. Damian survived the ordeal, the other guy, not so much.

Marisa knew Damian as a charming and engaging lover, but she also knew he would never hesitate to kill or destroy anyone who got in his way or tried to take him out of the game. She was realizing he may love her but that he would also lie about anything, maybe even his love for her, to get what he wanted. Marisa was a little afraid of what Damian was capable of, but she still loved him which, for now, was stronger.

"Damian, do you love me?' Marisa asked as they both sat on the two metal chairs facing each other.

"Of course, I do. I just need to know everything you told the government so we can avoid more complications. I want to spend the rest of my life with you but we have to get you out of here first, and you have to be honest with me."

Damian knew from his own sources that Marisa was lying to him about the extent of her cooperation and disclosures. He did care about her, but he could not risk his own death, or worse, going to prison. Damian sat quietly, knowing that what was to come would solve all of his problems with the Vasquez family.

During their visit Damian spoke romantically of the life they would soon return to, grand trips to Saint Tropez, the French Riviera, the Tuscan region of Italy, and other exotic destinations. Looking into Damian's eyes Marisa listened to him describe the dreams to come. His words were just like the beginning of their relationship. He swept her off her feet and into an international world of luxury and crime.

• • •

It was September when Damian first came to Caguas, Puerto Rico. He was charming and easily made friends at the local restaurant and bar buying drinks and telling stories of foreign places he visited. The day Marisa walked into the bar to find her brother, she immediately saw him. He stood out with his broad shoulders, six foot frame, blue eyes and dark brown hair. His clothes matched his physique and clung to his body showing off his assets. He was the only one at the bar she didn't know. He was vibrant and had the whole place talking and laughing at his stories.

As she walked up to her brother at the bar, she spoke cautiously to Damian.

"Hi, do you speak English?" she said to Damian with a grin.

Though Marisa's parents refused to learn English, the schools taught it as a second language. At home, Spanish was spoken to honor the independence of islanders who still believed statehood would ruin the Puerto Rican culture, a culture that had long ago assimilated to the American way of life. Marisa preferred English.

"Yes, I do and I can see you do as well." Damian replied.

"Si, yes, I speak and understand English. My name is Marisa." She gave William a hug and a curious look as if to ask, *"who is this guy and why are you with him?"*

"Can I buy you a beer, or should I say Cervesa?" Sticking out his hand, the charmer introduced himself. "Damian Garrison, such a pleasure to meet you Marisa."

"A beer will do, thank you."

William told Marisa that he was sitting at the bar, his favorite hangout, when Damian walked in with a motorcycle jacket on and leather pants. At first Damian kept to himself but after a couple of beers Damian started talking to him more openly.

"I see you met my brother," Marisa said.

"Oh, yes, we've met. William has been entertaining me with stories of some of his youthful exploits. Your brother is quite the adventurer," replied Damian.

With great emphasis William informed Marisa with three beer induced bravado that he could do what he wanted. He raised his glass and asserted his status.

"Marisa, my wonderful and beautiful sister, I am twenty-one now and I am my own man. Now when I do crazy things they call me an adventurer, a risk taker, someone to watch, but when I was younger I was called a hellion. I am ready to fly the coup so to say. Damian has told me of new adventures that are at my fingertips if I want to join him."

"Join him in what?" Marisa asked cautiously.

"Well," William replied, "Good question. I am not totally sure what Damian here does. I don't remember him telling me."

With that William and Damian both let out a bellowing laugh. Both had had too much to drink, Marisa thought.

All Marisa could do was shake her head with resolve. "What nonsense are you two talking about? You both are drunk and we do not know Damian well enough to engage in such musings. Please don't fill my brother with ideas of things he cannot do or have. What do you do, Mr. Garrison?"

Before Damian could reply William downed another beer and started slurring his words."Sissss, you ssshould see Damian's tricked out Harley Davidson outside. That issss what I want."

"I brought it over from the mainland." Damian offered, avoiding her second question for now and William's drunken bravado. "William should have one. For that matter, so should you. In fact, you should have anything and everything you want, you are beautiful."

This pick-up line was used on her all the time, Marisa thought. She knew her five foot seven frame was desirable, but she never felt anyone genuinely wanted to get to know who she really was inside instead of just her body. -

Damian had been looking at her features all night. She was dressed in ankle skinny blue jeans, heeled blue sandals, and a soft green shoulder drop cotton shirt that enhanced her sparkling hazel eyes. He was smitten with her enough to move forward with a date.

"Look," Damian said. "Let's talk for a while. If you don't like me, no harm done, but if you do," he said with emphasis on the *do*, "then maybe you will let me take you to dinner."

"Right now, you are just another drunk guy in the bar looking for a woman to bed." Marisa said with contempt.

"Just give me some more of your time, I promise you will like me," Damian replied.

Marisa could not help but smile at his persistence. "Ok, one more beer but you and William do not seem to need anymore." It surprised Marisa that after she said this, Damian only drank sparkling water the rest of the night. Just maybe he was a decent guy.

Marisa spent the next two hours that night listening to William and Damian share stories of escapades and travel. To Marisa it felt good to laugh and meet someone from anywhere outside of Puerto Rico. Damian had been everywhere. It was easy to get caught up in the magic of his stories and the life that he had built for himself with fast cars, boats, houses and travel all over the world. It sounded unreal. He never once mentioned how he earned the money to support this life he was describing, all he said that night was he was in international shipping and sales.

The night went by quickly. Marisa was captivated by someone who was not an island boy but a real man exuding confidence and charm. He was charismatic and full of life. Damian said she was beautiful. Even if at first she thought it was a line, no one ever said that to her not even her mother and father. Any of the local boys who said she was beautiful were only looking for sex, not love. Marisa was ready for something different, and Damian was starting to make her feel special. Marisa remembered his first date invitation that same night at the bar.

"Marisa, would you consider a more formal date in San Juan, dinner and dancing perhaps?" Damian asked.

Marisa did not hesitate, she hungered for a change and maybe, just maybe Damian was the one to bring it. "Yes, I would like that," she told him. "Will we be riding the Harley parked outside?"

"We can, but a car might suit you better for this occasion. I will pick you up on Friday at eight."

Marisa remembered the feelings she had anticipating a date with Damian. She was warm inside and her heart beat faster. She told herself to slow down and not get too excited. It was after all just a first date and he was not planning on staying in Puerto Rico. At that time in her life she thought she would never be able to leave the island, though she longed for a life anywhere else.

That night at the bar, Damian finally said goodnight to Marisa and William and roared off on his Harley.

•   •   •

All of these memories seemed so long ago. Marisa's mind wandering was her escape from the reality of her surroundings. She was barely listening to Damian as he returned from describing a better life together to describing the final details of his plan.

"Marisa, are you listening to me? Do you know what you have to do?"

"Yes, Damian, we have been over this before, keep your voice down or the guards will hear us."

"Don't tell me what to do Marisa, this only works if you do your part and make sure you are where you need to be and on time."

Marisa knew not to argue with Damian. His temper became apparent some six months after they were dating when he told her what he did for a living. If things were not running smoothly he looked for someone to blame. Off-loaders were particularly good targets for his anger when they were moving too slowly. Little did they all know that he always had his own man present at all of the off-loads to report on their success or failure. Marisa would more often get the brunt of his anger if she was the supervisor for a failed off-load. Though he never hit her, he came close many times. If things went well he would reward her with a nice dinner or jet off to another romantic getaway. On those trips he treated her as if she were the princess of everything. He trusted her, and she chose to live for the love not the anger. She was also not ready to let go of the money and the fast life.

Marisa returned to listening more intensely to Damian's plans. "I know you and William can make this happen," she interjected to whatever Damian had been saying.

"Yes, we can but you still have to do your part with Barrett. You need to get me her information. You have to make the introduction and get her on board."

"I will Damian, I have been talking to her every day. I think she will be interested in what you have to offer."

As Marisa ended her prison visit, Damian kissed her softly on the lips. Not too long but long enough to remind her of what they had together. He told her he would see her soon.

"I love you," Marisa said as Damian walked out of the visiting room. Damian did not reply.

· · ·

Once Marisa left the visiting area she was strip searched before being allowed to get on the elevator to her floor. It was humiliating. Taking her clothes off and having to bend over to have her cheeks spread to see if she was taking anything illegal to her cell block was degrading. Even without the search, there were ways to get contraband, especially drugs, into the prison. Even guards would help if the money was right.

As Marisa walked to the elevator to return to her cubicle, her mind again returned to the pleasant feelings she had when she kissed Damian, trying to shut out the oppressive sights and sounds of prison, hoping he still loved her.

The Friday of their first date was special, but Marisa had little to wear. She and her family were on welfare assistance. She had no real skills or work experience even though she was 26. There were no jobs for her without additional education. She did not want to be a secretary or answer phones all day; she wanted more, and maybe Damian would provide something more than a life of poverty. She chose her Sunday dress which itself was old. It was a simple pale blue sleeveless sundress with white and yellow flowers. She wore an old pair of white open-toed low-heeled sandals. She was excited and nervous at the same time. She was afraid he would see her for the poor country girl she was and always would be.

The night of their date Damian drove up in a rented black Mercedes convertible with the top down. His dark brown hair slicked back with just a wisp falling on his forehead; he was tan as if he had been at the beach all day. He dressed in black pants, a white T-shirt tailored to his fit body and a black jacket. She so wanted him to be more than just another date.

When Marisa walked out of her small brick house where she still lived with William and her parents, there was an ocean breeze blowing her hair off her shoulders. She could see in Damian's eyes that she grabbed his attention. She remembered him walking up to her with his eyes wide open. He told her she reminded him of the French girls he dated in the past. At that time Marisa had no idea it was only a few weeks before they met that Damian had been in France with someone else. For the first time, she remembered feeling special and hoped Damian meant it when he told her she was beautiful. Her heart was filled with anticipation. She had never been on a date with a man with money. She not only knew she wanted him but had a feeling he wanted her as well. She remembered every word they said to each other that night and what they did.

Damian got out of the car and presented Marisa with a gift, perfect for that evening.

"You are so beautiful" he said. "I brought you something special to wear. I hope you like it."

Damian pulled out a beautiful white shawl made from Italian silk. It was perfect to match her blue dress and white shoes. Suddenly her old dress sparkled with a waterfall of luxury.

Marisa remembered Damian opening the door to the convertible for her to get in and driving off to San Juan on a breezy tropical night in September. No one had ever done that for her before. After a fine gourmet dinner they left for an afterhours bar and dance club. He could do a fast, smooth salsa or glide across the floor with her in his arms to a slow song. That night he made her feel as if there was no one else on the dance floor but her. Damian told Marisa of a lifestyle she only dreamed of, yachts on the French Riviera, dinner in Paris, and summers in Switzerland. When the evening was over Damian never asked her to return to his hotel, he took her home and kissed her goodnight. Marisa never wanted the evening to end. Damian treated her as if she were the queen of the night, a Spanish Cinderella.-

"Will I see you again?" she asked, uncertain of his response or interest.

"Of course." He replied, "I'm here for the next two weeks so let's do something fun tomorrow. See you around ten?"

She was so excited that night, sleep never arrived. For the next two weeks, she and Damian were hardly ever apart. They slept together on the third date and she never looked back. She knew he was the one. Marisa was in love with a dream.

•   •   •

Marisa's roommate came in from supper, interrupting her thoughts. Marisa seldom ate the meals brought on trays to the floor. If you ate the food you sat on metal seats attached to metal tables in the middle of the two rows of cubicles. Marisa preferred to eat snacks in her room that she could buy from the prison commissary. She avoided the prison food as often as possible. Feeding several hundred inmates three meals a day from government surplus cans and meats is just not healthy, and any hot food usually arrived cold.

"Marisa, how come you didn't eat tonight. Are you alright?"

"Not hungry. Yes, Cindy, I'm alright just tired of this place, the noise, the unhealthy conditions, and no fresh air, nothing to do."

"I can't take much more of this myself. My lawyer said I would be going home on bond soon."

Marisa knew that Cindy would not likely get a bond for armed robbery of a bank, even if she was just the getaway driver. Cindy had been there for ten months with no bond. It was her attorney's ruse to keep her spirits up. The crimes Marisa committed were serious and she was a flight risk so she never expected to get bond and Jan never lied to her about it. Marisa thought, *what would Jan say now if she knew what I was about to do?*

Cindy left to go the eating area, where after supper, inmates were allowed to watch TV or play cards and some old board games. Marisa lay on her bunk and again distracted herself with the wonder of the first night Damian made love to her. She had been on a cloud for the two weeks he was in San Juan as Damian spared no expense in courting her.

He knew how to please a woman. On their third date his love making enhanced her female responses like she never imagined. Softly he touched her breasts, filling her with warm shudders of early pleasure. Gradually he slid his soft hand down her stomach to her female essence, caressing the warm pleasure he felt there. His tongue was magic, touching her ever so slightly as he slowly moved her beneath him. He worked to ignite her desires. He was an unselfish lover and gave Marisa more pleasure than she could have hoped for. She would be satisfied only after he stopped moving just at the moment she reached her release. Their love making so intense that they could barely walk the next day. Marisa let out a quiet sigh, releasing the tension of memories gone wrong and falling asleep, the noise of the prison silent in her mind for now.

•   •   •

Before Jan picked up the phone to speak to Assistant United States Attorney Jake Hardin, she reviewed previous events that occurred in court last week. Jan had flown up to New York for a pretrial conference with the prosecutor and Judge. Marisa's judge in New York was not sympathetic.

"Your Honor, the government is acting in bad faith." Jan told the judge. "They agreed Ms. Cardosas would not have to cooperate against her brother.

Now they have changed their minds and are requiring her to turn her brother in to even be considered for a lower sentence than life in prison."

"How would it hurt at this point to bring the brother in since the government already knows about his involvement through other intelligence? Where is the brother anyway?" Judge Norris inquired of Jan.

"The brother has not yet been apprehended or indicted your honor."

The judge, to her credit, asked the government why it would not give Ms. Cardosas and her brother a deal to get to the source of the drugs without putting both family members at risk of a lengthy sentence.

Jake Harden gave a simple reply. "Because they are both guilty! We will give some consideration to the brother if he can help us get the source of the drugs and break up this large international drug operation. However, for now no deals until we hear what they both have to say."

"Sorry," Judge Norris said, "it is within the government's sole discretion to decide who gets a deal and to bring that deal to me, including any recommendation for a mitigated sentence for cooperation. I do not see any bad faith for now."

Jan and Jake left the courtroom together. "Jesus, Jake," she said, "Give them a deal they can live with, not die from!"

"Look this is a big international case. I will give Marisa and her brother a deal if they both cooperate fully. We are always looking for the main sources of drugs no matter what country they come from, so this is an important case to the government. We need the source and the corrupt agents. See you in court next time. Let me know if you want to accept a plea for now and see what shakes out with her cooperation before sentencing. No promises without the brother."

Jan looked out her office window. These were Jake's last words to her. She simply could not get Marisa to turn her brother in or ask him to come in and face the unknown. Her hands were tied and she didn't like it.

"Jake is on line one," David advised through the phone intercom.

"Hello."

"Jan, how are you?"

"Well I am okay but we need to work out a deal for Marisa. What if she convinces her brother to come in, what would you do for him?"

"First get him to agree to come in with or without his sister's approval. I will discuss with you my impressions and then you can talk to her. He will need his own attorney at that point, if he even comes in. If Marisa continues without him she is looking at thirty years under the federal sentencing guidelines. With her cooperation and not the brother's I would consider thirty."

"Okay. I don't like the options but I understand you are not going to budge without the brother. I will see what I can do. Have a nice weekend."

"You too Jan, always a pleasure to speak to you."

Frustrated she saw it was after five. "David, I'm leaving, I have had enough drama for this week. See you Monday."

"I am right behind you."

Jan left her office wanting to make the Friday night date with Kellie her priority. She put some romantic music on her Lexus radio to mellow out before getting home. It was just a few miles, usually two songs on a CD or the radio, depending on traffic. When she arrived she met Ranger at the door, or rather Ranger met her. This was Jan and Kellie's child, a 3-year-old male German Shepherd. He came from a home that could not keep him due to his size but he was a perfect fit for them and a good guard dog.

"Hello Ranger," Jan said as she entered the front door. "Sit, good boy." Ranger knew his training and how to get pets and a hug, and sometimes treats when he responded to commands.

"I love you, Ranger," Jan said. Being greeted by Ranger was one of the best parts of coming home. It was like magic. A smile appeared on Jan's face and the work and city jungle she just came from slipped away.

"Hi, babe," Kellie called.

"Are you talking to the dog or me?" Jan said to Kellie who had come out from the kitchen.

"I've already gotten my welcome home from Ranger. I was hoping for a little more human affection this time."

Jan held out her hand to Kellie, drew her close and planted a long lingering kiss on her soft lips. This was the main thing that could change a bad day to a good one, knowing she was with the love of her life, touching her, holding tight to her strong body still in shape from her days as an FBI agent and their mutual love for hiking. The embrace lingered as the stress of the day drained away and they breathed together. This was Jan's family, the most important part of her life.

"Glad you could make it early tonight," Kellie said as she walked back to the kitchen. "We are having some fresh salmon, angel hair pasta with capers and a light cream sauce for dinner. Interested?"

"Why of course I'm interested, how nice of you to cook." Jan replied.

"Oh that's not all I have planned, honey. Why don't you go upstairs and change into something more comfortable while I attend to dinner. When you come down I will have a nice glass of pinot noir waiting."

Kellie thought about how much she loved Jan as she continued to cook dinner. Jan had a big heart and was her best friend. She was the one person in her life that made her the happiest. She helped Kellie make sense out of life's unexpected twists and turns. Despite being pretty, her personality made her even more attractive. She was always helping others, was kind and a good lawyer. Jan and Ranger were her family. They met on a cruise nine years ago and she never looked back. Jan had a big family and welcomed Kellie the first time they met her as if she had been in the family for years. That helped fill the hole left by her own family. Kellie shook her head and took a sip of wine to get back to being in the moment. She would be lost without her.

Jan dropped her briefcase on the foyer table, kicked off her shoes and took them up to the bedroom on the second floor. She loved the home they lived in. The ground floor was perfectly set up with an open floor plan so the living room and dining area could be seen from the kitchen. They had a lot of friends who would come to dinner or just drop in to chat. The second floor had an office, two guest bedrooms and a big beautiful master bedroom and bath. The king size bed in their room was perfect for two people and a big dog. Jan threw herself on the soft bed cover, looked at the ceiling and sighed with joy over her love for Kellie and the life they had built together.

•   •   •

Damian and William worked in an old barn on a farm in upstate New York about fifty miles outside the city. Damian had his bodyguard arrange to rent the barn for two months while they put their plan into action. The barn was located in an area that was isolated. The family who owned the land was no longer living there and was trying to sell it as a whole or in pieces but the market was soft, and it sat for months without interest. When Damian approached the family and offered them twenty thousand dollars for two months' rent of just the barn they did not hesitate to rent it to him. No questions asked, all cash, under the name of David Stone. Upstairs in the barn was a loft style living area with a small kitchen, dining table and two beds. There was a small stand-up shower and toilet separated by a curtain. This was the perfect place to implement the plan and what it would require.

Damian and William had the plans and materials for a special kind of craft that would allow them access to the roof of the prison where Marisa was incarcerated. The homemade aircraft they intended to use for the escape was delivered to the farm in the name of one of Damian's many aliases, this time Greg Jones. They needed to be close to the city to make the flight on one tank of fuel.

The ultra-light helicopter was supposed to hold two people. The weight of the passengers and the fuel had to be carefully calculated. They needed to fly to the city, pick up Marisa, and fly out to the pickup location undetected. Damian had his own ideas as to how everything needed to come together.

"William, you have been working on this for almost two months. Is it ready to fly yet? We are running out of time," Damian said impatiently.

"I know, I know," William replied.

"We need the cover of darkness and clouds to pull this off. If we have to delay any longer we could lose our window of opportunity."

"Damian, I am doing the best I can. I am just finishing up a few adjustments to the engine but it is fully assembled. You keep your mind on what you have to do. Have you arranged the money drop-off for the guard? Is the pickup vessel ready? Stick to what you have to do and I will do my part."

The strain between them was getting worse. Damian knew things about William that kept him from trusting him fully; after all William was responsible for getting Marisa arrested. William had no idea that Damian knew what happened that night.

"It will work; I'm just making the final modifications and will test it out before we have to fly into the city. You just make sure you remain within walkie talkie range once we get going," William added.

"Stop telling me what to do as if you are leading this little adventure. If it wasn't for me, Marisa would be spending the rest of her life in jail and you would be dead. It is your mistakes that got us into this mess in the first place. I will do my part. Tomorrow morning, I meet the prison guard for the money exchange. The flight details are up to you. Don't screw this up, William!"

"Stop worrying, I have this. Be careful, the guard still works for the government."

"Yes, I know. I am ready for the meeting. We need this guard to pull this off."

William knew Damian was right about it being his fault they were in this mess in the first place. His goal was to make it up to his sister and Damian. He regretted his behavior that night and his constant drinking to deal with the stress of the drug trade.

Damian had his attorney look into the background of some prison guards to find one that was having problems with the staff or who might be in financial trouble. He was lucky to find Andrea Barrett, one of the guards that worked on Marisa's floor. She was having financial problems due to lawsuits she kept filing against the government over not getting promoted. Marisa was instructed to talk to her as much as possible and to befriend her in a way that would get information and see if she was vulnerable. With all of the attorney's fees used for fighting employment discrimination she was on the brink of bankruptcy. She was more concerned with the principle of her fight than the reality of winning.

Marisa told Damian about Andrea's constant complaining of the unequal treatment she received and how it changed her. Andrea was bitter and angry over false promises that even after ten years on the job she was still not moving up. She needed money, so she turned to helping other inmates by getting paid hundreds of dollars from family members to bring in cell phones and cigarettes without detection. She avoided bringing in drugs as that was more easily detectable since the prison got a drug sniffing dog to stand at the front gate while everyone checked in for work or a visit. She was desperate for money or a way out of taking care of prisoners the rest of her life.

Marisa told Damian that she was able to gain Andrea's trust when she told her she knew about the smuggling she was doing for inmates for a pittance compared to what she could offer her. Once she had Andrea's trust she told her that her boyfriend had an offer of more money than she could make doing illegal contraband smuggling. She did not tell Andrea about her plans, just that there was a lot of money in it for her if she met with her boyfriend. Until Marisa was sure she would do what they all needed her to do, she would not disclose any details. For Andrea she had already been corrupted, so the offer of a large sum of money was a lifetime of freedom from the revolving door she felt stuck in. Andrea was told that Damian's name was Greg Jones. Marisa got Andrea's cell phone number and gave it to Damian.

Damian got ready for his meeting and made the call. Marisa told him Andrea was interested in meeting him to see what he had to offer. "Hello, Andrea, this is Greg. I know you have spoken to Marisa. Can we meet? I am on my way into the city. I can meet you in front of Carnegie Hall in about an hour."

"I'll see you there, Mr. Jones. I sure hope this is for real and not some set up with the feds," Andrea replied.

"No, I assure you it is not set up. Please call me Greg. I want to help Marisa and her case, and I think you can help me do that. We need to meet in person. It will be worth it, trust me."

"Ok, I am curious. Don't be late, I only have an hour for lunch."

Damian drove past Carnegie Hall thirty minutes before they were scheduled to meet. He enjoyed going to such places instead of meeting in a cheap hotel or restaurant parking lot like common drug dealers. He thought of himself as a corporate executive running a successful company. He pulled his car into a parking spot a block away to avoid being memorable to anyone who might be near when he met Andrea. He walked the block to the meeting spot in front of the Hall and saw a woman who matched the description Marisa gave him and a driver's license photo he obtained from a DMV friend on his payroll.

Andrea saw the stranger approach her fitting the description Marisa gave her. They had never met in person so Andrea was a little nervous. "Are you Greg?" She asked skeptically.

"Andrea Barrett?" They shook hands.

They stood outside in the early spring weather; sun shining, about sixty degrees, talking in soft voices as people hustled passed them. He filled her in on the hope to break Marisa out and what was at stake. The streets of New York are always busy and no one pays attention. They were just another set of faces in the crowds that walked by.-

"I will give you one hundred thousand dollars, in cash, if you help Marisa execute her part of our plan," Damian said.

"I don't want to be arrested for this Mr. Jones." Andrea replied cautiously.

"There is no chance you will be arrested if you stick to the plan." Damian assured her. "You could walk away and turn us in if you wanted to, but you are still talking to me so you must be interested. I have enough dirt on you. I know you bring things into the prison and I have inmates ready to turn on you if you double cross me."

That was not all Damian would do but he did not need to go there as Andrea was already interested when he mentioned the money. -

"Are you threatening me Mr. Jones? No one would believe a bunch of inmates."-

"The accusation alone could be career ending. All that fight for nothing."

She thought this through. "I am interested. But, I hold the cards here despite what you think you know about me, Mr. Jones, or Greg, whatever you want to be called. If I accept your offer how will we make this exchange?" To Andrea this was enough money to quit her job and get out of the city. She always wanted to move to the country in North Carolina or if she had to leave the United States she would go to Belize or Costa Rica where her money would go farther. This was her chance, and she decided to take the risk.

"Come to my car. It is at the end of the block."

Together they walked to Damian's car and got it the front seats. Damian handed her a duffle bag filled with fifty thousand dollars in fifty and twenty dollar bills.

"This is a down payment. When the job is done you get the rest. You may count it if you wish, Andrea."

"No thanks, I figure it is all there since I control the outcome of this little adventure. You better be good for the rest."

"This is true but in the end we have to trust each other."

"I could walk away with the fifty thousand and not do anything but put Marisa in the hole and leave her there. I will expect the rest the next day. How do I reach you?"

With cold and calculated words Damian told Andrea, "No one will get hurt if you do your job. Yes, you could double cross me, that is up to you. We can meet again the next day at noon, at this same location to get the remaining balance."

Andrea took the duffle bag and got out of the car. No other words were spoken. She knew she had enough money to get away even if she did not get the rest of it. The total would be over two years of a tax-free salary. She contemplated, only for a moment, leaving now and never going back to work.

Damian drove back to the farmhouse outside the city. If their plan worked, Andrea would never have to worry about the government or a promotion again.

•　　•　　•

Jan and Kellie left the weekend open for themselves. It was Saturday and it was raining. They talked about Kellie's trip and Marisa's case off and on all day in between movies and relaxing. Jan could not get Marisa off her mind.

"Kellie, as a former FBI agent, what would you do if someone cooperated, like Marisa, but would not give up a close family member like her brother?"

"Marisa faces a difficult choice," replied Kellie. "I would have recommended she get some credit for her cooperation so far and see what she would be able to do on a continuing basis. The problem with my strategy is that it would not be my call, but the prosecutor's. They really need the brother to corroborate her story. We were trained never to believe one informant without more support or evidence they were telling the truth. She knows a lot more than the mules or off-loaders, so the information she has already provided may be useful but it does not get to the suppliers or the head of the snake, so to speak."

Jan thought about that and what if she had to disclose something intimate or personal, or for that matter illegal, about Kellie, would she do it? "You know babe, I would do the same thing as Marisa; disclose what I know but keep you out of it."

"Thank God I don't have to worry about that!" Kellie said with a laugh. "What exactly has Marisa said?"

Jan told Kellie more than she should have. Being partners somehow made the concept of attorney client privilege not a concern; she trusted Kellie's opinion and discretion. Plus, this case struck a nerve with Jan. When she was a teenager, her big sister, Amanda, had gotten into some trouble with an older man who led her down a dark path. Her sister ended up getting arrested delivering drug money for her boyfriend. She was not involved in his dealings but her misguided love for him made her agree to help on a couple of occasions. A friend of the family was the officer who arrested her. Luckily, he brought her home without pressing charges, and she was scared enough to turn her life around and cooperated against the boyfriend. Jan saw a lot of Amanda in Marisa.

"Marisa is in deep with a very serious drug family. They would kill her and her brother if they thought for a moment she tried to cooperate against them."

"Does Marisa's brother know she has cooperated?" asked Kellie.

"Not that I know of but I am afraid there is someone who does; a guy named Damian Garrison. He has called me once or twice trying to get information from me on Marisa's case. I have not told him anything but I feel he thinks he is entitled to know. Marisa told me that Garrison also goes by the name David Stone and is her boyfriend. On his last call, he got angry and threatened me. He said he could make my life a living hell if I did not release the government's discovery information to him. Marisa is my client and I am bound ethically not to release this information to anyone but Marisa and even then, I can only discuss the information with her but not give her the documents. I told this Garrison guy what I was ethically required to do, but he did not seem happy about it."

"Why didn't you tell me this before?" asked Kellie.

"Because I know you would want to do something about it, and I could not let that happen. I should not even be telling you this now."

"Jan, you know I would never breach your trust or that of your client's. I can tell it is getting to you but being threatened is not something you should ignore." Kellie's FBI instincts heightened with this conversation, she wanted to protect Jan from any possible danger.

"I know. I just don't know who this Damian Garrison is, but Marisa is in love with him. I need to know more about him if I am to help her. Kellie, can you check him out with your security skills and past FBI contacts?"

"I can try but if anything happens to you I will hunt this Garrison guy down and kill him myself."

"I know you would, baby. I know you would."

After that they both decided to stop talking about work and instead opened a bottle of wine and talked about anything but work. Jan and Kellie were finishing off their second glass of wine when Jan suggested they get more relaxed. "How about getting into the Jacuzzi after dinner? The rain has stopped and it is a cool evening."

"Sounds good to me," replied Kellie.

The Jacuzzi was warm and inviting; the September rain had stopped and left a slight chill in the air. The Jacuzzi never failed to relax them both and quiet the chaos of the world around them. Adding the wine to the moment only made it better.

As Kellie watched Jan's naked body slip into the hot water with her she was reminded why she loved her life now more than ever. Kellie came from a broken family, a sister who died of an overdose and a mother who became emotionally absent when her sister died. Her father just left after that event and never came back. She fended for herself and made a decision at a young age she would not become a product of her family history. Joining the FBI gave her discipline and perspective. Jan gave her a life and a family. She and Jan had been together for nine years. She was happy in this moment remembering that she left the FBI when they asked her to move to the Detroit office to be a supervisor. To her, it was a step up, but in the wrong geographical and emotional direction. She did not want to ask Jan to leave her law practice or the life they had made together in Atlanta. She resigned from the FBI instead. It only took four months for her to find a job with a company called Security Acquisitions, Inc. She was making three times as much as she had made as an agent. It wasn't the perfect job, but it was a job that kept her and Jan together. This was more important to her than a job she loved. Her own family motivated her to find a better life for herself and she did. Any sadness from her family history was washed away with a feeling of warmth from the water, the wine and this moment with Jan.

As they sat in the Jacuzzi the warm water and wine relaxed them both, Jan could see Kellie was lost in her thoughts. She decided to enhance the Jacuzzi experience and turned her undivided attention to Kellie.

"I want you to occupy my mind and body, distract me." Jan said with a smile.

Kellie smiled with anticipation. She always welcomed time for romance and tenderness shutting out the worries and cares of their jobs. They put their glasses of wine on the deck, turned up some romantic Pandora tunes on her smart phone and embraced each other in the warmth of their surroundings intoxicated with romance and love.

•   •   •

"Marisa, wake up! We are having a shakedown!"

Marisa was deep in sleep when Cindy started shouting at her to wake her up. Shakedowns happened frequently and unannounced but not usually at four a.m. on a Saturday morning. The object of such intrusiveness was to catch prisoners with contraband. Even having an extra plastic can of tuna from the commissary could get you in trouble but most of the time the guards were looking for weapons or drugs.

"Stand at the opening of your cubicle!" a voice yelled over the PA. Marisa and Cindy complied as did all of the prisoners on the cell block.

A guard came into their cubicle and started turning everything upside down: the beds, books, clothing, everything. When the guard got to Cindy's bed he flipped the mattress over. He then shook out her pillow from the cotton casing and started examining the stuffing. He felt something hard inside the stuffing. He tore the pillow open near the seam where there was a small opening. Inside the pillow was an Aspirin tin with six Tylenol with codeine tablets in it. Suddenly the guard yelled for backup and demanded both Cindy and Marisa get on their knees on the hard floor facing the wall.

"That's not mine!" Marisa protested.

"I keep them for headaches," Cindy said without much emotion considering the terror of a shake-down. Getting in trouble for having contraband meant isolation in the SHU.

"Shut up and put your hands behind you," replied the guard. "Both of you!"

Marisa and Cindy were hauled off to solitary confinement until an investigation could be done to find out how Cindy got the medication into the prison. Marisa was a suspect just for being Cindy's cellmate.

Marisa realized Cindy always complained of headaches while they were incarcerated together but figured it was because of the stress and noise of the prison environment. No doubt she got the codeine from a family visit or brought in by a sympathetic guard. Marisa could not blame her since medical care at the prison was slow and everything was diagnosed as malingering. Marisa saw injuries and illness go unattended until someone got so sick they had to be taken to the hospital, looking close to death. Most were removed from their cubicles never to come back. Right now, however, none of that mattered as they were both in trouble and this was not good.

Marisa knew once you were in the SHU it could take months to resolve any misconduct investigation. Marisa pleaded with the unit manager.

"Mr. Simon, you know I had nothing to do with this."

"Be quiet. Until we can sort this out you know the rules, everyone from the suspect cube is placed in the SHU."

"But this could take months and Cindy admitted the medication was hers!" Marisa's pleas went unanswered. The solid steel door to her tiny one person cell slammed shut. She stood in an eight foot by six foot room even more claustrophobic than her cubicle. Inside the cell was a stainless steel sink, steel toilet with no seat cover, a thin blanket and pillow folded at the end of a steel bed with another two inch mattress. There was not even a sliver of light from the outside, a virtual coffin.

Marisa feared the worst. She had no way to tell Damian or William where she was. Solitary confinement required twenty-four hours of lockdown with no freedom to move around in general population. She would be fed through a slot in the door on a tray with even less desirable food than the commissary. Usually a bologna sandwich on white bread twice a day, cup of apple sauce and a powdered drink with no nutritional value. Marisa knew she could not handle these conditions and worried she would miss her window of opportunity to escape. She tried to hold back her panic.

All their planning was now at risk. To make matters worse, the weekend staff was limited to one guard in the SHU; so no case manager would be available to resolve her case until Monday. Marisa sat on the steel bed and cried, the life she knew was over. She would die in a small cold room with no natural light.

•　　•　　•

Damian sat on the bench in the barn looking at William's creation. "Have you tested this thing yet?" Damian asked.

"Yes, the best I could without drawing too much attention to us. I pulled the Ultralite out into the pasture and started the engine. I lifted off the ground about three hundred feet and it worked perfect. The only concern I have is the weight of two people and the fuel calculations."

Damian needed this to work. "You already know how to fly helicopters. All those lessons you paid for better pay off."

Damian was getting worried about Marisa caving in to the government's pressure to save her brother. He also worried about William. He was weaker than his sister and made stupid mistakes. Damian could not risk getting caught or Marisa telling the Feds his whereabouts. Though Marisa was smart, William was often careless and endangered them all.

"You know I love your sister. You don't think she would reveal anything about me or the business do you?"

"Why do you ask me that?" replied William. "I know my sister, she loves you and would do anything to protect you and me."

Damian was getting more and more paranoid with what the government might know. He would have to leave the country before they could find him if Marisa broke. He knew from his own attorney that Marisa already told them more than just what happened the night of her arrest. He paid for the information from agents he knew were crooked. The agents in the islands could access information on international investigations easily. The problem was this. Jan Bergin did not know Damian was paying Marisa's legal fees. He felt that if he was paying she should tell him what he needed to know. She was being obstinate about discussing the case with him and he did not like it.

"I trust her." William added.

"I am not so sure. From my experience when someone is facing life in prison they will do things they never thought they would. You trust her because she is your sister. But, I know that love isn't always enough."

"Is that what you have done with my sister, told her lies to get her to do what you want? What do you think she would do?" William inquired.

"Cooperate for a lower sentence. I know the family I work for would not hesitate to kill someone who cooperated against their own. Hell, they would kill me just because I trusted her and worked with her. I can't afford to worry that I might be killed because of what Marisa might say."

"She would never turn me in." William was certain Marisa would protect him.

"No, William, I agree, she would never turn you in. I am not so sure about me or the others she knows about. She knows more than anyone else I have worked with. I was a fool and told her too much during our time together."

"She can be trusted. Besides, if we get her out everything will be as it was."

Damian did not reply. He knew nothing would ever be the same again.

•　　•　　•

Marisa could not help but wonder what had become of her dreams. Her thoughts drifted as she sat in the cold dark cell tears streaming down her face.

Meeting Damian was the best and worst thing that ever happened to her. He was smooth. He gradually gained her trust and led her into his dark world of drug trafficking. She went willingly and blindly, she was in love with him and eventually, the money. She had more cash than she knew how to spend despite buying luxury clothing and cars. She asked herself, was it all worth the risk?

The first job Damian gave her was to pick up the off-loaders and take them near the drop sites. Only when she had all the off-loaders, did Damian tell Marisa where the off-load site was. Later he trusted her enough to tell her this during the pickup process. The off-loaders would get paid in cash for their work taking the drugs off the boat and putting them in a van someone else would drive to the site. When the off-loading was complete the workers would be picked up in a second van and transported to the closest town to get to their homes on their own. They never knew where they were going until the last minute. Damian knew each of the off-loaders by name, phone numbers, home address and family information. He would use throwaway phones for every deal and threw the phone into a canal or the ocean when he was done. One off-load could net the average off-loader up to five thousand dollars for just two or three hours of work. Damian would give them false identifications in case they were stopped and told them to identify themselves as construction day workers if anyone asked.

"Hey, Marisa, you want your lunch tray?" came a voice from outside the cell.

"No, I am not hungry right now."

"Suit yourself. I will be back with a dinner tray later."

Usually inmates from the kitchen delivered the meals but Marisa had no idea who was talking to her since she could not see them. The only comfort she had was to keep her mind occupied with the details she knew about Damian's drug operation. Thoughts seeped in, she knew that this information might help her get out of prison. She did not want to think about this option too much, but the thoughts were there.

Damian was good at what he did and she admired that in him. He ran things like a fine-tuned business. He was careful to use the same workers on a regular basis but no more than five per off-load. The money was good, and paying in all cash allowed the off-loaders and their families to live under the radar of immigration enforcement. He had a group of loyal workers. Damian made sure all his regular off-loaders knew he would kill them or their families if they ever exposed him. He had killed a few off-loaders due to carelessness or just talking too much. The rest were afraid of him, but wanted to keep working for him.

Lying on the hard bed, Marisa remembered that in the beginning Damian treated Marisa like any other employee, guarded against showing any favoritism because of their relationship. He made her earn his trust, and she did. She was dedicated and learned everything so he would trust her, not only in love, but in business as well. She found that the business of drug smuggling was not what she enjoyed as much as the skills she was learning. Be organized, on time, and dedicated. Due to her loyalty, Damian eventually told her about his business model and the drug family he worked for in Colombia. It was one of the first times Damian had let his guard down. Damian told her that she proved to be a formidable partner in his crimes. She recalled how happy she was to be working and making so much money. The love was icing on the cake. How she let this all take over her life in this way was something she could not grasp.

For her part, Marisa started making ten thousand dollars a load for doing the pickups and drop offs. She did this several times a month before she was promoted to supervising an off-load site with William. Damian was never around during these events in case something went wrong; he told Marisa that he had other duties. When Marisa was arrested she was making over two million dollars a year in cash. William was riding her coattails as her assistant, sharing her profits and making some extra as an off-loader when he felt like it. Marisa never said no whenever William wanted to catch a ride for an off-load. She kept him in money and he spent it as if there was no tomorrow.

Marisa made more money in three years than she ever imagined, going crazy buying things she had only dreamed of as a young girl. She bought new clothes, a car and traveled with Damian around the world. He had her believing she was doing the right thing by telling her how much he loved her and that without all the money they could not enjoy the good life together. Life moved too fast before Marisa's arrest, now it was moving too slow. Marisa's thoughts were suddenly interrupted by someone yelling at her from outside the cell.

"Marisa, Marisa, how long have you been in the SHU?"

Marisa thought she heard the voice of Andrea Barrett, she had lost track of time and had no idea how long she had been in the SHU.

"Hello, is that you Andrea? I have been in here since four o'clock this morning. I need your help!" cried Marisa through the metal food slot she opened with her hand.

"I just started my shift. We have to get you out of here. Let me see what I can do."

"What time is it Andrea?" Marisa asked.

"It is close to eight in the evening."

Marisa never noticed that the dinner tray was sitting on the food slot. She never heard anyone deliver it.

"We don't have much time."

"I know, but you will have to be patient."

Those were the last words Andrea said as she walked away. Marisa had no idea if she would do her part in helping Marisa get away.

Just after midnight on Saturday was the best time to pull off Damian's plan, fewer guards and no administration for the weekend. Marisa knew that this night had to be perfect for everything to go off as planned. No matter what, she needed to be out of solitary confinement before midnight, or she would spend the rest of her life in prison.

"Marisa," Andrea said through the small food slat in the door, "even though Cindy confessed, the only way I can get you out of here is with the warden or assistant warden's permission and neither of them are here today. I will have to call them or get someone to help. This will take some time but I will be back to get you one way or another, sit tight."

In the SHU you are left in isolation with nothing but your own mind to save you or destroy you. All sensory perception is lost. Marisa was having trouble breathing and staying calm.

"Ok, but hurry, I have to get out of here!"

Andrea heard Marisa yelling but did not understand her as she was already on her way out, the metal bar doors separating the SHU from the general population slamming shut as she left.

Marisa needed to contact Jan. "I need to make a phone call to my attorney." Marisa cried through the food slot to the guard on duty at the end of a long hall of similar cells.

"I will bring a phone to the cell door," Officer Johnson replied. Attorney access was vital and most of the guards, if they could, would help a prisoner in the SHU make at least one call to their attorney, but no one else.

Officer Johnson brought the portable phone to the cell and opened the door so Marisa could use the phone and Johnson could still see her. She could only call approved numbers. Damian's number was forwarded through his Attorney's office to his cell phone. Damian's on-call attorney in New York was corrupt enough to set up a call forwarding system to Damian, making it look like she was calling an approved attorney. Johnson knew Marisa had two attorneys on her call list, one in Atlanta and one in New York; he did not know the one in New York was also Damian's attorney. Attorneys' numbers are easy to get approved and they are unmonitored calls.

"What number are you calling Marisa?" Johnson asked.

"My local attorney since what has happened here can be handled more quickly by my local counsel." Marisa lied about the call but the number that would show up in the computer would be to the local attorney's office.

Johnson opened Marisa's cell door. "Stand at the door to use the phone so I can see you." With that Johnson sat the phone on the outside of the food slot.

Officer Johnson walked away so he could not hear Marisa's discussion with her attorney but could see her. Marisa dialed Damian's lawyer's number that would connect to Damian's cell phone. "Damian, this is Marisa." she whispered.

"Are you crazy? Why are you calling me now, no names!"

Marisa was surprised at Damian's response. "I know better than to use a monitored phone. Officer Johnson let me call my attorney, but I wanted to hear your voice. I miss you terribly. I am in trouble here; they put me in solitary confinement."

"How the hell did that happen! Never mind. I don't want to know the details. Can you get out in time?"

"I think so, Andrea came by and said she would help get me out. I want to speak to William." Marisa said.

"He's busy. Let me go, we need the time to prepare. See you soon my love. Don't call me again."

Damian disconnected the line. He was not happy about her call. She could tell his voice was more condescending than loving.

Marisa noticed that Officer Johnson was not watching her so she dialed up Jan's home office number. The answering machine picked up.

"Hello, this is Attorney Jan Bergin. No one is here to take your call right now so please leave a message and we will return your call as soon as possible.

"Jan, this is Marisa. Just wanted to see how my case is going. If you don't think the government will give me a good plea deal let's go to trial or I will do something else to help myself."

Marisa hung up the phone. She wanted to tell Jan what was about to happen but Marisa was afraid Jan would try to talk her out of the escape and she did not want anyone to think Jan had anything to do with their plans. It was crazy dangerous. What fool would try what she, William, and Damian had planned?

•   •   •

At seven p.m. Saturday night Damian examined William's work. "Not bad. I like what you've done. Why don't you take a break? I will wake you in a few hours when it is time to go. You need the sleep."

"Thanks, I could use a power nap. This Ultralite helicopter has the necessary lift and fuel capacity to make the trip. It has two lightweight nylon seats, one for me with the joy stick for steering, pedals for lift and a seat behind me for Marisa. I will be able to fly in and pick Marisa up on the roof of the prison if the guard does her part."

Damian waited until William went up to the barn loft to rest before looking over William's handy work and making his own adjustments to the Ultralite helicopter. At approximately 9:30 p.m., Damian woke William. "Here buddy, a cup of coffee to help you wake up."

As he sipped the welcomed hot coffee, William started the engine of the

Ultralite. "Hurry up William, you will be late; we have no window for errors."

"It will take me about two hours to travel the distance to the prison. Damian, you need to be at your pickup site by midnight; so worry about what you have to do not what I need to do. I am on it. I want Marisa out as much as you do."

"Don't tell me how to do my job!" shouted Damian. "If it wasn't for me, both you and Marisa would either be dead or living in poverty." Damian was tired of it all. He had to work too hard to clean up this mess, but he had little choice if he was to find out what the government knew and who he needed to kill so the Vasquez family would not find out about his mistakes.

"Damian, you recruited us and changed our lives. I am doing this for you and Marisa," replied William.

"You wanted what I had to offer. Now let's get Marisa and stop fighting." Damian was tired and needed this night to end the way he had planned.

William saw an increase in Damian's anger towards Marisa's carelessness in getting caught. Damian constantly worried about what she had told the government or was willing to tell them to save herself and her brother. Damian trusted no one when it came to saving his own neck. William knew Damian's distrust was not unfounded. People were careless and would betray anyone for their own freedom, a common practice if you got caught in a criminal enterprise. If Damian knew how his own carelessness caused Marisa to be arrested he would have killed William already. .

The Ultralite was quiet and only made a small buzzing sound. William took off and let his thoughts wander as he flew the Ultralite towards the night lights of New York City.

William remembered the night he and Marisa got caught. They, or rather Marisa with him in tow, were supervising an off-load of three hundred kilos of cocaine and ten thousand pounds of marijuana. The workers were moving slowly and daylight was coming up fast. This was the fourth such off-load they had handled in only three months, but the biggest one yet. No off-load site was ever used twice. When the drugs eventually hit the streets, once stepped on, were worth millions of dollars. The wholesale price of an uncut kilo of cocaine could be twenty-five to thirty thousand dollars. One kilo of cocaine could make multiple kilos. It was just like a corporation; supply and demand would set the prices.

Flying the Ultralite was easy after flying helicopters, but it was slow going. His thoughts of that terrible night consumed him. William had been drinking before he got to the off-load site the night Marisa was arrested, something Marisa knew he did frequently but never told Damian. Marisa's van and William's car were parked near the off-load site in the southern Florida intercoastal area of Boca Raton. Every now and then Damian moved down the coast of Florida for a change of location or up to northern New York, particularly in the summer months when the flow of drugs was more consistent. The name of the town, Boca Raton meant the mouth of the rat, an ironic setting now. The site could not be seen from the road. There was no moon, and it was late. The area was isolated but every now and then a car would drive by. The small boats came one after another to a rented dock behind a home used only in the winter by some Canadians. Damian found out about it through his sources, a perfect location on the canal for a late night off-load. Most of the neighbors would be in bed and if anyone saw them they would think they were coming back from fishing overnight.

William always drank when he accompanied Marisa on an off-load. He already had three beers before he arrived, and when he got there he threw the last empty bottle on the road before turning down the drive to join his sister behind the empty house. An unsuspecting motorist ran over the shards of glass from the broken bottle and punctured a tire. Pulling over, the driver got out of his car to change the tire. When he was finished he stood up for a cigarette and saw some suspicious moving lights behind the house where they just finished the off-load. He thought that it was too late for anything lawful to be going on, and radioed the police. The guy assumed there were high school kids behind a vacant home looking for trouble. What he saw was the small boats pulling away from the dock after they had finished the off-load. The driver changed his tire and left the scene, not wanting to get any more involved.

The off-load was complete and the small drop-off boats were gone before the police arrived an hour later. Only William and Marisa remained cleaning up anything that might have dropped during the off-load process. Marisa sent William with the off-load van and was just pulling out of the area herself in William's Cadillac Escalade when she was pulled over by the police.

William found out later that during questioning, the police became suspicious of Marisa's explanation that she was there to look at the area for a possible house purchase. A drug dog was brought to the scene and alerted to the cocaine and marijuana smell in the area. Marisa was read her rights and arrested. At first, she gave them an alias but did not have the alias identification on her. Eventually she gave her real name. A search of the area revealed no drugs but even the cops could smell the marijuana. The DEA was called to the scene. They found muddy footprints in the ground behind the house matching the shoes Marisa wore the night of her arrest along with many other footprints. The DEA wanted to know what was going on and who was there with her. She said nothing at first but the agents knew her name. When they looked her up, they connected her to the crew in New York who got arrested in the harbor incident. Someone in that crew knew her, so New York claimed jurisdiction, tying her to a conspiracy that went from New York to Florida. She was pressured to cooperate and instead of calling her attorney, she started talking when they promised her if she did cooperate things would be easier for her. Her comments were limited but she ended up giving the feds enough to charge her and use what she said against her if she went to trial and testified on her own behalf. When she finally retained Jan, the damage had been done. William was the cause of this mess and it continued to occupy his mind as he flew closer to the New York skyline.

Damian always had his own man on the job, not for the money but to be his eyes and ears so he knew what happened. His most trusted bodyguard and friend, Caleb Simmons, was known to William and Marisa as off-loader number five. No names were ever used, only numbers. He was always on her crew and Damian told her he was his most trusted off-loader and strong enough to help with big loads. He frequently heard Marisa talking to William trying to get him to focus on his job. She would get angry over his carelessness but would cover for him as she had all their lives. At this moment William knew he had to save his sister no matter the consequences. This was his mess and he needed to clean it up.

After William lifted off into the dark, partially cloudy sky, Damian was supposed to drive to New York harbor to do his part in rescuing Marisa.

William traveled above the ground at about fifteen hundred feet at thirty-five miles per hour. It wasn't speed he needed but maneuverability and he needed to conserve fuel. The lift blade created the ability to go up or down while the smaller thrust blade behind the Ultralite pushed him forward. He worked the joystick and pedals with the rudder for lift and direction.

Flying was what William enjoyed most. It took him away from his wasted life. He felt bad that he placed Marisa in such a dangerous position and wanted nothing more than to get her out of prison. The lawyers could not do it, so he was determined to. He promised himself he would get out of the drug business if he got through this. He was also afraid Damian would never let him or Marisa out. They were now liabilities. They knew too much.

•   •   •

"Marisa, how you holding up in there?" Andrea asked through the meal slot.

"Andrea, for God's sake, get me out of here!"

"I'm trying but I have to get approval from the Assistant Warden on call tonight. I faxed the paperwork to her home. She is looking over it as we speak."

No one ever told Andrea of the escape plan, only the part she was to play for the money she got. Marisa had to rely on Andrea and that she would do what she promised Damian.

"What time is it?" Marisa asked.

"It is close to eleven, why?"

"I have to be out of here before midnight, you know that." Marisa was getting stressed out not knowing if she would make the pickup.

"I know," Andrea replied. "I am doing all I can to get you out without causing more suspicion."

•   •   •

It was almost eleven p.m. and William was still twenty miles from the prison. The headwinds were stronger than he thought. He was trying to concentrate on the goal, but his mind kept wandering. He felt stupid for believing Damian's stories of travel and wealth. He had never worked a legitimate day in his life. Everything Damian told him sounded so easy. He loved the money but hated the process he went through for it. He also knew he was a drunk and had to change that part of his life as well. He had been reckless and care-free to the detriment of those he loved most.

Damian told him that he could get rich quick if he would do what he was told and come with him to the mainland. He saw how his sister liked Damian and wanted her to be happy. She fell in love with the man while he fell in love with the devil's business. William promised himself if they all survived this that he would start a new life. No drugs and no alcohol. Maybe he could find a job flying helicopters for tourists in Hawaii. He had enough money to get away from this life for good.

• • •

It was now 11:10 p.m. and Marisa was still in the SHU. She was getting fran-tic. If she was not on the roof before midnight, William would not land. They only had one shot at this. The roof was used for giving the prisoners time out-side. They could walk around the roof or play basketball in a fenced in area but there was another area not fenced in for staff to sit and watch the prisoners during their recreation. The fenced area was ten feet high but nothing on top. There were no guide wires overhead. The recreation area was large enough for the Ultralite helicopter to land and take off. No guard tower was needed due to the height of the building and the fence. The air conditioning units on the roof made enough noise to muffle the soft propeller sounds of the Ultralite. This left about three thousand square feet of open space. It would take skill but someone could land a small Ultralite helicopter in that space. Marisa knew that if anyone could do it William could. The one thing he was really good at was flying helicopters. He loved them and took lessons for two years hoping one day to have his own.

Time was ticking away. Marisa bent over and push her face up to the food slot to look at the clock on the wall near where Johnson's desk was located. It was not easy but she could see the hands moving, 11:32, 11:33, 11:34. Marisa's heart was pounding in her chest. She was so nervous she could not breathe. 11:36, 11:37.

She began banging on the cell door and yelling through the food slot. "Someone let me out. I can't breathe! Please let me out!" It was now 11:38.

"Marisa, you need to quiet down." Officer Johnson said.

"I want to get out of here. Where is Andrea?"

"I'm right here Marisa."

Andrea walked into the Special Housing Unit. She could hear Marisa yelling from the hall. It was 11:40.

"Johnson, open the door and let her out." Andrea demanded.

"Andrea, you know I need top authority to do that, and you're not it."

"Johnson, just do it! I have a signed confession from Cindy that Marisa had nothing to do with the codeine pills."

Andrea ranked higher than Johnson, but the rules were clear. Authority to release a SHU prisoner had to come from the top; it was 11:43.

Marisa was getting claustrophobic. *Dear God, I have to get out of here,* she cried to herself. 11:45.

• • •

Using his phone GPS, William could see he was close to the prison. He was beginning to maneuver around the skyline of Manhattan. There was no moon and no rain. There was some low cloud coverage which was beginning to break up. He needed to get Marisa out of there before the clouds moved out. The lights of the city gave him enough reflective light to help him see where he was going. It was 11:45 and he was still three miles away.

• • •

"Marisa, I am putting a call in to the Assistant Warden at her home."

"Andrea, hurry!"

Johnson was curious as to why the rush. After all it was just another prisoner in the unit and it was the weekend.

"Why do you care about Marisa, Andrea?"

"Because she has been in the SHU since early this morning and we know she had nothing to do with Cindy's drugs."

"Look, you do not run the prison even though you think you should. I know about your lawsuits," Johnson said.

Andrea was furious. She wanted to put him on report. No one was supposed to know about her ongoing feud with the administration. She looked at her watch, it was 11:50. Andrea picked up the phone and dialed the number to the Assistant Warden on duty.

"Ms. Haynes. This is Andrea in SHU. Do I have permission to release Marisa Herrera-Cardosas?"

"If I have seen all of the paperwork, go ahead. Make sure the final investigation report is on the Warden's desk in the morning before you leave."

"Thank you, Ms. Haynes. Would you tell this to Officer Johnson?" She handed the phone to him.

Johnson listened to Haynes and reluctantly opened the cell door. Marisa had that wild eyed look of an animal caught in headlights. Her prison clothes were soaked from nervous sweating. Time was running out.

"Marisa, come with me." Andrea said. It was 11:55.

"Andrea, I can hardly breathe," 11:56.

"Listen, I am going to take you to the roof. I have to leave you there and go back to the unit. I can't afford to be caught with you. If I am in the unit when they do the 12:30 a.m. count it will look like I brought you back to the cubicle and you left on your own sometime after you were released from the SHU."

"Andrea, was this whole thing a setup?"

"Yes. I knew about Cindy's pills on Friday. I saw them before but did not write her up. It gave me the out I needed to get you to the roof. After I met Damian, I figured I could set up the shakedown and get both of you into the SHU. It would be easier to help you this way."

Marisa and Andrea got on the prison elevator on the fifth floor headed for the roof. It was 11:57.

• • •

Damian was at the Marina at 11:45. He was running late. He passed security at the dock by flashing a marina identification he had secured months ago. He started the two seventy five horse powered engines of the nineteen foot Boston Whaler and put the throttle in neutral. The boat was outfitted to look like a fishing vessel with a center console and rod holders attached to the small roof over the console. He bought the boat a few months back just for this purpose. He needed to get out of the Marina without being heard. He put the throttle forward ever so slightly to avoid causing a wake and to limit the noise. The engines of this boat were designed for speed. Once clear of the Marina he pushed the throttle forward and sped off into the darkness and turned off the boat running lights.

• • •

When Andrea and Marisa got to the roof, Marisa was out of breath and close to panic. They were running late and would be out of time for their window of opportunity.

• • •

William could see the roof of the prison. He followed the road below the buildings leading to the front of the facility to aim his sights.

• • •

"I am leaving you here Marisa," Andrea said. "I have to get back to the unit. Don't forget count begins at 12:30. If you are not in your bunk, a second count will occur to be sure you are missing. You will only have five to ten minutes after the first count to be gone. The alarm will sound and all hell will break loose. Good luck."

"Thanks Andrea, thanks for everything."

"No thanks needed, I got paid well."

With that, Andrea left the roof and went back to the unit. She could only hope her story would work and she would not be arrested herself. If they just allowed her to leave she could disappear on her own terms.

•　　•　　•

Damian was within range of the harbor drop zone, they were running late. Damian had to keep watch for the harbor patrol. He turned off the engine to avoid making too much noise. He did not want to attract attention from one of the many container ships waiting in the harbor for clearance to off-load merchandise at the port or the harbor police that regularly patrolled the area.

Damian turned up his walkie-talkie. "Unit one, this is unit two, come in."

"Unit one, this is unit two, come in!" he repeated in a whisper.

William heard Damian through his ear-piece and pulled his walkie-talkie out of his flight jacket pocket. "This is unit one, over."

"Are you near the pickup spot? Is the package ready?" This code, if over-heard would not be unusual in New York. It would sound like a twenty-four hour delivery service was working on a late package pickup and drop off.

"I am close. I will let you know when I have the package."

•　　•　　•

William was trying to maneuver the Ultralite over the roof of the prison. The winds picked up and he was having difficulty controlling the joy stick. His decent was slow but he steadied the Ultralite to drop down in the small open space on the roof. He saw Marisa in the shadows near the door.

"Marisa, let's go!" he shouted as he landed.

"William, I can't believe you made it." She ran to him and gave him a hug.

"Hurry, we don't have much time. Get in the back seat and put this life vest and helmet on." It was already 12:10, past the arranged pickup and takeoff time. They were dangerously close to prison count which would set off alarms once they found Marisa was not in the SHU or her general population cubicle.

As William was trying to take off, the engine sputtered and died. He had idled back too much and the engine shut down.

Marisa screamed, "William, we are running out of time! Get this thing started!" She did not think she could handle one more crisis. Her nerves were already raw from the stress of being in the SHU all day, and they were running out of time.

"I'm trying." The more he tried, the more flooded the engine was getting. "Listen," William said. "I have to let this thing rest for five minutes before we can restart."

"We don't have five minutes!" Marisa cried. It was now 12:15.

•   •   •

"Unit one, this is unit two. Where are you and do you have the package?" It was Damian trying again to reach William and find out where they were.

William had turned off his walkie talkie to avoid any additional distractions when he approached the roof and made his landing.

Marisa's heart began to pound so hard she thought it would come out of her chest.

At 12:20 William tried the engine again. It took three tries but he got it started. "Let's go!" Sweat was pouring down William's face. Those five minutes seemed like hours. Marisa could hardly breathe.

Marisa prayed the Ultralite would fly with both of them. William was saying the same prayer. By the time they took off and were on their way; it was 12:25 and the prison count would begin in five minutes.

•   •   •

"Unit one to unit two, come in, over. Unit one to unit two, come in, over!" Damian was not happy as he had been drifting in the area of the pickup spot for fifteen minutes. The boat lights and engines were off but he was drifting too far from the pickup location. He had to start the engines and slowly move the boat back into position. He left the boat in idle to keep the noise of the engine to a minimum but still running. "Unit one, come in!"

Finally William replied. "This is unit one. I have the package. We are on the way!"

•   •   •

William had more trouble keeping the Ultralite on course with two people in it. He could not get up over a thousand feet above the top of the prison building. He had to weave his way around other buildings to get to the harbor.

Marisa was scared out of her mind. This was insane, she thought. She tried not to look down.

"Marisa," William shouted over the wind ; "when we get over the drop site I will go as low as I can! You will have to jump into the water! I will follow you after I know you are down!"

"OK, but, William, I'm scared; it seems too high!"

"I know, but this will work. You will hit the water hard but you will be okay! The vest will keep you afloat and the helmet should help protect your head when you hit. I will try and get you down to fifty feet above the water."

•   •   •

Andrea made it back to the cell block around 12:15. She and one other guard were all that were on duty. Officer Albertson was asleep at Marisa's general population cell block officer's desk when she returned. All was quiet and most prisoners were asleep. No one noticed her return. Prisoner count was every four hours and the twelve thirty nightly count was about to begin. Two lieutenants appeared on the floor to address the count and take the information once count was complete. They did not have to wake the prisoners, just check their beds. They would then go to the next floor and so on until all prisoner units and the SHU were checked and all inmates accounted for.

Andrea and Officer Albertson began the count precisely at twelve thirty. Each prisoner should be in their bunk. Only Cindy's name appeared as being absent for cause on the sheet that had the inmates' names on them for count to be tallied. Andrea made sure the tally sheet did not reflect Marisa's absence.

Andrea gave the count sheet to the two lieutenants. "There are twenty-eight prisoners on this floor, we should have twenty-seven and we only have 26 without Cindy," said one of the lieutenants. "Who else is missing?"

"Let's do a quick recount," Andrea offered. "I want to be sure we did not miss someone." She was trying to buy some time before all hell broke loose.

"Who is missing?"

"It looks like Marisa Herrera-Cardosas," replied Andrea. "I brought her back from the SHU about thirty minutes ago."

"Check the bathrooms again and if she is not there, sound the alarm."

•   •   •

Marisa and William were over the harbor near where Damian was to pick them up. William could not see anything. He knew he had to trust Damian and jump when they were three miles off the Manhattan shoreline. William and Marisa had light sticks attached to their life jackets. If Damian followed his coordinates he would see them in the water. William maneuvered the Ultralite to about fifty feet above the water. This is as close as he dared to get and still control his maneuverability.

They were approaching the drop off. "Marisa, get ready. "Go!"

Marisa turned sideways and looked down, she was scared to jump.

"This is as close as I can get!" shouted William. "Go!"

Marisa had to tell herself it is either jump or die or go back to jail. None of these choices was what she wanted. The water seemed so far and it was dark. Her fear threatened to stop her from jumping..

"Marisa, you have to jump!"

She could hear William yelling on one side of her brain and the other side was telling her you are crazy; you are going to die. All the preparations for this moment seemed lost. She knew she had to muster the strength to jump. With a deep breath she turned to get in a position to leap out of her seat.

As Marisa turned to jump, she saw some wires connected inside the seat pocket behind William. As she tried to look closer, William shouted again.

"Go Marisa, Go! Hurry! I can't hold it steady much longer!"

William turned around and with one hand on the joy stick he took his right arm and pushed her out of the Ultralite and into the water.

As Marisa went over the side, the sudden loss of weight rapidly jolted the Ultralite another two hundred feet upward. William was having trouble correcting his lift and placement over the drop site where he pushed Marisa out. He was now away from the drop zone. It would take too much time to turn and try to locate the spot Marisa jumped, so he tried to lower the Ultralite to a safe distance from the water so he could jump as well. This was the plan and the Ultralite would fall in the water and disappear just like them. No one would know what happened or even where to look for Marisa. William thought that once he was in the water and broke the light stick Damian would see him and pick him up. He did not think he was far from where Marisa should be.

Marisa came down hard in the water and lost her breath. The life jacket kept her on the surface bobbing like a cork at the end of a cane fishing pole. She was listening for William's splash as she was afraid to shout his name for fear someone might hear her.

"William?" she whispered breathless, "William?" She could hear the soft propeller sounds of the Ultralite in the distance. Suddenly, there was an explosion above. Marisa looked up to see the Ultralite burst into flames..

"Oh God! No!" Marisa cried. "William, William" she cried louder, "answer me, please answer me!"

Marisa scrambled to take off her helmet. She broke her light stick and shook it until it was shining fluorescent green. She swam frantically around the area where she had been pushed into the water by William. She could not see anything, just falling parts of the Ultralite still burning about two hundred yards away. She realized this could be seen by anyone nearby including harbor patrol. She was struggling to get her bearings and emotions under control. Surely William had already jumped, she thought.

"William, William, where are you?" She kept calling his name, each time getting louder, there was no reply.

Damian was a hundred yards away from the drop area. He could see one light in the water using night vision goggles. He knew he would not see a second light.

• • •

Andrea watched as the prison escapee protocol began to unfold.. All efforts to find Marisa were exhausted and the only conclusion the staff could draw was that Marisa had somehow escaped or was hiding. They just did not know how she could escape.

The prison SWAT team had been called to the scene and were questioning everyone, especially Officer Johnson from SHU, and Andrea. Someone from the SWAT team would be going over camera tape from the SHU and the general population floor where Marisa was housed. They might not yet look at the roof top cameras as no one was supposed to be up there or have access to the recreation area.

"OK you two, tell me again, what happened?" asked Captain Dean to Johnson and Andrea. "When was Marisa released from the SHU?"

"I got Marisa around eleven fifty-five and took her back to her room on my floor," Andrea replied.

"Andrea called the acting assistant warden on duty who told me Andrea had permission to release Marisa to her cell block," Johnson offered. .

"Johnson, did you have something in writing about her release?" asked Captain Dean.

Johnson was feeling pressured. "Look, you are not going to pin this on me. Andrea is the one who has problems here. I talked to the AW and she said everything seemed to be in order; so I released her to Andrea's custody."

"We have not been able to locate or call Assistant Warden Haynes. For now both of you are suspended. Finish all of your paperwork and go home until you get a call from the Warden or the internal investigation team."

Captain Dean was efficient with his time. After questioning the staff he sent his men and women out to the perimeter and roof to gather physical evidence and any information from street witnesses and the cameras. It never occurred to them that the locked door to the roof would be a point of concern until they actually went up there. How Marisa got a key to the roof would become the focus of their investigation.

"Captain, we have found a spot of fuel residue on the roof!" shouted one of his men.

•   •   •

Marisa could hear the engines of the speed boat nearby.

"Marisa! Marisa! It's Damian. I can see you." Damian was shouting over the noise of the engine. Damian was within twenty feet of Marisa. He put the engine in neutral and glided to where Marisa was floating in the water. "Where is William?"

"I don't know. Did you see the explosion? He can't be dead, he just can't be!" cried Marisa. "What went wrong?"

"I saw it. I have no idea what went wrong." Damian acted equally surprised and upset.

Damian allowed the boat to drift closer to Marisa. He could see she had been crying. He helped her into the boat from the ladder in the stern used for swimmers to be able to get in the boat from the water. She was wet and cold.

"Here, take this blanket, my love. We have to get out of here; the harbor patrol probably saw the explosion and will be coming to this area to investigate."

"Damian, I can't leave William! He is out here somewhere. Help me find him!"

"We can't wait any longer. Along with the explosion the prison will be looking for us and will likely notify harbor patrol."

"No, I have to find him!"

Damian knew this could happen. He tried to comfort Marisa but he also had to get them out of the immediate area. He put the boat in full throttle forward and sped away to Stanton Island towards the Bayonne Bridge. The best chance of him to escape was to get closer to New Jersey. His contacts would be waiting near the bridge to pick him up. Before they got there they would have to ditch the boat and swim to the shore line at the bottom of the bridge.

Damian was running without lights when he started to hear the sound of a siren in the distance. He looked around and could see the harbor patrol siren lights in the distance. They were about two miles from the original drop site.

Damian slowed to idle and looked through the night vision goggles. The harbor patrol was headed for the area where the Ultralite exploded. He did not have much time.

"Marisa, we have to keep going. When we get to the bridge I will sink the boat. We have to get out and meet our connection on the Willowbrook Expressway."

"Who will be waiting for us?" asked Marisa.

"My bodyguard," Damian replied.

• • •

It was now two thirty in the morning and Andrea was worried as she left the prison. Nothing seemed right. She was sacrificing everything in her life for what? Had she done the right thing for herself? These questions scared her, she did not want to go to prison and she had seen how bad it can be as a guard. She had to get out of there as it was too late to turn back. No one would ever believe that she had nothing to do with the escape since she was the last one with Marisa when she left the SHU. She knew she had little time to get the rest of her money and disappear forever. She could only hope the life she was headed for would work out.

As Andrea walked briskly to the subway station, a lone hooded figure quietly stepped out from behind a building and shot her once in the head before she could react or even knew what happened. No one was around and the silencer kept the gun shot muffled. Andrea's body was cradled in his arms as she fell. He carried her body into the alley. Wearing gloves he took her wallet and key to her apartment. He then gracefully lifted her body into a large trash bin. He knew that when, or if, the body was ever found that it would look like a robbery. He went to Andrea's apartment and took back the money Damian had given her. Services rendered, fee paid.

• • •

"Damian, where are we?"

"We are close to the shore. Get ready to jump in. We have to swim to shore as it is too shallow near the shoreline to get the boat any closer."

"I am tired and can't believe you left William behind! I hate you!" Marisa cried.

"It could not be helped. You should be thanking me for getting you out of prison. Do you have any idea how much money I had to use to get people to help us? Don't be so ungrateful. Look, I know it is hard right now, but maybe William is alive. We just can't go back and look for him now. Relax, you know I love you." Damian had to calm Marisa down to finish his plan. He would tell her anything to keep her going. He could not afford to get caught. The remote explosive behind William's seat was supposed to take care of both of them.

•   •   •

At three fifteen in the morning Jan's phone rang.

"Hello?" Jan said trying to clear her sleepy mind.

"Attorney Bergin? This is Captain Dean from the Federal Prison in New York. Your client, Marisa Herrera-Cardosas, has escaped."

Jan sat straight up in bed, waking Kellie. "What is it?"

"Marisa escaped," Jan whispered to Kellie holding her hand over the speaker of the landline.

"Captain, what happened?" asked Jan.

"We believe Ms. Cardosas was picked up on the roof by some kind of light helicopter. Some wreckage has been located by the harbor patrol. Do you know anything about this, Ms. Bergin?"

"Of course not, I am as surprised as you are, Captain Dean."

"We are going to investigate this matter thoroughly, so if you know anything I suggest you tell me now." Captain Dean said ominously.

"That sounds like a threat Captain." Jan retorted.

"No ma'am. Everyone is a suspect. If she gets in touch with you, please contact me." With that, Captain Dean gave Jan the phone number to his office and hung up.

Jan wrote the number down on a pad next to the bed and told Kellie what happened. "Marisa escaped from the roof of the prison. They think she did it by helicopter."

"That seems awfully hard to do," said Kellie. "I'll get up with you and put on some coffee."

"No honey, you go back to sleep, your flight to Colombia is not until noon."

"I'm already awake and can finish my packing while you pace. I know you too well Jan, you will wait for a phone call."

•   •   •

Marisa was physically shaken, cold, and angry. "What happened out there Damian? What happened to William?" she shouted.

"I know as much as you do," he answered. "I don't know what happened, maybe some kind of malfunction with the wiring, something he missed. We have to keep going or we will both be caught."

"William is too good with electronics and helicopters to have just missed something. What was that I saw behind William's seat on the Ultralite?"

"I have no idea what you are talking about. It was probably part of the fuel line."

Marisa knew something wasn't right; Damian's answers were too quick to focus on a possible cause for the explosion. She started to look around the boat.

"What are you looking for, Marisa?"

"I'm looking for a flashlight." She lied to him at that moment out of fear that he did something to William and was about to do something to her.

As she looked around, Damian was busy getting the boat closer to shore so the swim to shore would be as easy as possible. Marisa was trying to see in the dark. She was holding the glow stick to help her see. The light stick was getting dim and was now giving off very little illumination. She wasn't sure what she was looking for but knew when she found it: C-4 wired with a triggering device and two remote switches.

"Damian, what is this?" she asked, pointing to the C-4.

Damian was concerned. "The explosives are to blow up the boat after we get out. The switch is so I can detonate the explosives from the water or shore."

"Why are there two switches?"

Damian did not answer. He pretended to concentrate on steering the boat to their destination. They had to hurry. In the distance they could both hear the sirens from the harbor patrol getting closer. They would be swarming the area after the explosion thinking it was another terrorist attack. There would now be an all-points bulletin out for Marisa as well.

Suddenly Damian turned around and pointed a nine-millimeter gun with a silencer at Marisa.

"What are you doing Damian?" Marisa froze, her mouth open.

Marisa's head had been spinning out of control since she got locked up in the SHU. Everything had happened so fast that her mind could not catch up to what she was doing. She had been going nonstop with no time to think. She lost her brother while escaping from prison. She tried to comprehend why her lover could have possibly killed her brother and now he was trying to kill her. She was wet, cold and confused.

"I'm sorry, my love. As much as I hate to, I must leave you behind. You are becoming a liability. There is too much at risk to keep you around."

Marisa realized that all of this was setup, masterminded by Damian from the beginning. She realized that after getting arrested, Damian could not afford to have her alive, much less William. She had been so naive. She loved him. She escaped a life of poverty for a man who told her breaking the law was worth it to be together. Somehow she ended up convincing herself that it was the only way she could get out of her life of poverty and isolation. She kept telling herself all that she had was worth the risks. Now it all seemed like a bad dream.

"Damian, please you do not have to do this," she begged. "I love you, and you know I am not going to do anything to hurt you."

"Well my love, maybe not, but that is not the issue for me. I just cannot take the risk and I needed to resolve the Vasquez family concerns about you after your arrest."

"Damian please!" Marisa did not know what to do.

"Hush now, I have to tie you up and am going to leave you on the boat. I have no choice. Killing you hurts more than killing William. William has been a screw-up from the beginning. I'm sorry, but it has to be this way. I will make it fast and painless. The harbor patrol will find your body and think you blew yourself up."

Marisa was in shock. Everything she had believed in, worked for, and loved, was gone, betrayed by her misguided dreams. She felt like she was watching a movie that was coming to a more horrible end than what was expected by the audience. She was a spectator to her own death.

Marisa turned to see the harbor patrol blue lights getting closer. They had sophisticate equiptment to see boats in the darkness. They likely saw their boat when they were looking around after the Ultralite exploded. In a split second and without thinking she grabbed her life vest and jumped over the side of the boat, back into the water. The cold water shocked her. She threw the life vest away from her so that Damian would have trouble seeing where she was using the night vision goggles.

Damian did not expect Marisa's sudden movement overboard. "Marisa, don't do this! The end will come no matter where you go. Remember, I can see where you are. There is no escape from the inevitable."

Marisa knew the shore was at least fifty yards away. Could she make it without her life vest? She had to try. She went under the water to swim as far as she could on a deep breath of panic. She zigzagged underwater to avoid coming up where Damian might expect her. Marisa held her breath as long as she could before surfacing. She could hear the bullets zip into the water nearby as Damian shot at the life vest. She took another deep breath and dove under again. She could not see anything in the dark night and murky water. Her heart was pounding in her chest as she tried to hold her breath as long as possible and headed in the direction of the shore so Damian could not see her with his night vision goggles.

•   •   •

"Damn!" Damian looked for Marisa with the night vision goggles but he too was running out of time with the harbor patrol getting closer. He found her life vest but she was not in it. He fired several silent .9mm rounds into the water where he hoped Marisa would be. He could not know if he hit her or not. He was running out of time and had to get rid of the boat and get to shore himself..

Damian threw the gun and night vision goggles overboard, grabbed the remote switches and slipped over the side of the boat. He swam far enough away from the boat to avoid being hurt by the explosion. He could not tell where Marisa was but he ended up swimming west under the bridge. He had no choice, as this was the side of the bridge that his body guard would be waiting for him. He waited long enough for the harbor patrol to get closer. Once he triggered the explosives, the harbor patrol boat would slow down to avoid the debris from the explosion, which would give him the extra time he needed to get away.

"This is Harbor Patrol, stop your vessel and come to starboard!" Damian heard the loudspeaker command but he had no intention of responding. He swam close to the shore, riding the current that would take him under the bridge before detonating the explosives in the boat. The harbor police were within two hundred yards of the boat.

Damian flipped the second switch on the remote and lit up the sky with fire and boat parts. He dove underwater to avoid any debris. It was more spectacular than he expected. Some of the explosion debris hit the harbor patrol boat which made them back off even more. .

Damian surfaced close to shore and climbed up the shoreline. He was cold and wet, but he had made it.

•   •   •

Marisa was struggling to get ashore. The current was strong and was pulling her under the bridge. She was tired and struggling but finally made it to shore before going under the bridge, she was exhausted. She pulled herself up on the grass and fell to the ground. She was out of breath, tired and cold. She saw and heard the explosion that was meant to kill her. She had to get her head in the game; she had just escaped from prison, jumped into the harbor from a helicopter and then from a boat her lover blew up hoping to kill her. Her brother was likely dead and she was alone. *What the hell do I do now?* she thought with desperation.

Marisa needed to get to the top of the bridge to get help. Though she was tired and cold she started jogging up the embankment. She realized she was still in her orange jail uniform. This would be a problem if someone saw her but she had no choice but to hope someone would help her and not know she was wearing prison clothes.

Marisa finally reached the top of the bridge. She stood at the end of the bridge for minute collecting herself. She could see multiple cars had pulled over and people staring below the bridge to see the fire. She realized she had to get out of the area. Soon the area would be crawling with cops and harbor patrol..

Prison clothes were always orange or khaki, depending on whether you were in pretrial proceedings or if you had already received your sentence and were on your way to another prison. The clothes they gave you were always too big, old, and worn by too many prisoners who had gone before. The clothes had the shape of hospital scrubs but had her name and prison number sewn on the front pocket. Marisa took off her orange prison top hoping her running bra would pass as part of a running outfit with her orange prison pants. No wire bras were allowed in prison and Marisa knew the modern way of exercising was with only a running bra and shorts. Being wet she hoped she would look like she had been running and sweating. She would have difficulty explaining why she was out in the middle of an interstate at four in the morning. She looked at the cars pulled over on the bridge, most everyone was distracted by the explosion in the harbor. She slipped up from the side of the bridge on the top of the embankment and started walking along the highway. She needed a ride and some money.

On the shoulder of the road were several cars. One of them a family style van with Maine license plates. Marisa knocked on the passenger side window. It frightened the women sitting there holding her child. She would not roll down the window.

"Excuse me, I could use a ride to New Jersey. My boyfriend and I had a fight and he made me get out of the car and took off. I have been trying to jog home but am getting tired. I'm afraid I can't make it back to the city. Could you give me a ride?"

The woman did not answer but shook her head no.

"Hey! Who are you and what are you doing around my van?" came a voice from behind.

Marisa turned to see a thirty something, six-foot two, two hundred pound half hippie, half yuppie, standing next to her. He had shoulder length hair and was wearing an Oxford shirt, khaki pants and Birkenstock sandals.

"I need a ride to the city. I had a fight with my boyfriend and he just pulled over on the interstate and pushed me out of his car. Did you see that explosion?" Marisa was trying to make small talk and give a plausible reason for being on the bridge and in the clothes she was wearing.

"Yeah that was something. We were on our way home from visiting relatives when we saw the flash from about a mile away. My wife did not want me to stop, afraid of terrorists."

Marisa was trying to be friendly. "I really could use a ride. I don't have any money to get a cab. I left my wallet at home. We were just going for a ride because neither of us could sleep. As you can see I am not carrying anything and in these clothes I sure don't look like a terrorist."

"I don't know, my wife will be spooked. We have our kid in the car."

"Look, I'm afraid to stay here and too tired to run. Just help me out, please." Marisa was getting desperate and she was telling the truth when she said she was too tired to run.

"Let me talk to my wife. Step back a little so she will open the window to talk to me. She already got mad at me for stopping and getting out of the car to see what was going on."

Marisa waited. She could hear some of what was being said. She could tell the wife was not happy. Marisa kept her eyes out for any suspicious vehicle or anyone approaching, she had no idea what vehicle Damian would be riding in.

"My wife is not too thrilled, but she agreed to give you a ride. She does not like going into the city at this hour in the morning. If you try anything …."

Marisa interrupted him, "Thank you very much for giving me the ride."

The sliding van door opened and Marisa took a seat behind the wife. Marisa did not want to give her real name. "Hi, my name is Christina."

"I'm Peter and this is my wife, Julie, and our two-year-old daughter, Amber." The wife was holding their daughter but just nodded and said nothing. "We will take you to the Marriott in Jersey City."

•　•　•

Damian was struggling in the current as he was swept under the bridge to the other side from where Marisa got to the shore. He reached the shore exhausted and cold, but alive. His grand plan worked for William but he was not happy about missing the opportunity to kill Marisa. He had to get to the top of the bridge to meet his ride out and his next move. The harbor patrol and Coast Guard were everywhere and soon local cops would show up on the bridge. He looked back one more time in hopes of seeing Marisa. This was getting even more messy and harder to clean up. He decided not to tell anyone about what happened to Marisa, except his bodyguard Caleb until he had more information. For now he could not afford to have the Colombians know anything different. Marisa knew everything, including information on the whereabouts of the Vasquez family.

Damian worked his way up to the top of the bridge, it was much farther than he expected so by the time he reached the top he was out of breath. He met his bodyguard exactly where he said he would be on the shoulder of the beginning of the Bayonne Bridge, coming off Willowbrook Expressway, southbound, pretending to have car trouble.

"How long have you been here, Caleb?"

"Only ten minutes but traffic is slowing down as they pass by so I don't want to stay her any longer. Someone may call roadside assistance and I am sure the cops will be coming as well. We need to leave now. I saw the explosion below and that will bring the cops down on this spot."

"William is dead," Damian told Caleb. "I am not sure about Marisa. I think we still have work to do."

Damian and Caleb left the area in an older model stolen blue Dodge pickup. It was four o'clock Sunday morning. They drove over the bridge and despite the early morning hours a number of passing cars had pulled over just before the toll plaza to see what had exploded in the harbor. New York is always on edge after nine eleven. It would be risky to stop and look for Marisa. Damian knew she was probably alive and had a pretty good idea what her next move would be.

· · ·

Jan went into her home office to pull up information on Marisa's case from her computer. She noticed the answering machine light was blinking. She pressed the button for messages and listened to Marisa's message. She never thought Marisa would try to escape, but she also knew Marisa would try to contact her.

"Jan, what are you thinking?" asked Kellie, bringing in two cups of coffee, dutifully followed by Ranger.

"I am worried about Marisa. I have never felt she understood what she had gotten into with this Damian character."

"He is bad news. I'm not sure it is even his real name." Kellie had been trying to help Jan with information on her case and this Damian character through old contacts with the FBI she had e-mailed over the weekend, but could find nothing on him.

"Honey, when do you leave for Colombia?" Jan asked Kellie.

"At around ten the flight is set for noon. Do you want me to cancel and get a later flight? I can stay an extra day to help if you need me to."

"No babe. Thanks. I hope Marisa will contact me, just not sure when or how."

"You can't help her now; don't be foolish. Here are the numbers where I will be in Colombia. Here is the satellite computer hook up code so we can communicate through e-mail and Skype when I am in Apartado and Turbo. Even though our base will be in Medellin, we will be out in these rural areas most of the time. Don't hesitate to contact me if you need to. Baby, I am worried about this; you could lose your law license. She is now an escaped felon and God knows what she did to escape from the federal prison in New York."

Jan was about to risk her career to help a client beyond simple representation. She would be walking in a gray area of the law but would try not to cross over the line from legal assistance and advice to criminal liability. She had to try and get her to turn herself in. Her escape is going to really mess up her cooperation credit and chances for a reasonable sentence. Marisa was not making her job easy.

• • •

Damian and Caleb turned around and headed for New Jersey. They kept their eyes peeled, but did not see Marisa on the other side of the expressway among the crowd watching the fire from the explosion. Caleb was Damian's trusted right hand man, confidant and bodyguard. He also would do Damian's dirty work when called upon to do so. Damian needed to get out of the United States but he could not leave without knowing Marisa was in his custody. He decided killing her may not be the answer. He needed to know what she told them and maybe at the same time take a look at the discovery documents to find out who else was cooperating.

"Caleb, let's ditch this vehicle, wipe it clean and get a limo to the airport. I want our private plane to Atlanta ready by first thing in the morning."

"No problem, I will have the plane ready by seven in the morning. What's in Georgia?" Caleb asked.

"All Marisa has left, her attorney," replied Damian.

• • •

"Christina, you must have run a long way after being thrown out of your boyfriend's car," Julie said with increasing suspicion to Marisa.

Marisa was trying to think of some kind of story to tell based on what she was wearing but could not come up with anything specific so she just said: "Yes, I was running to get away from him if he decided to come back." Not totally untrue, she thought.

"Do you have any money for a cab?" Without trying to explain herself further, she hoped they would give her the money. She was hungry and needed to call Jan.

"No," replied Julie, but Peter seemed to want to help.

As they pulled up a small local hotel downtown, Peter took out a ten dollar bill and said, "that's all I can spare, maybe you should get a job or another boyfriend." Peter was giving advice where none was asked for, but then again Marisa could not actually tell them who she was or what she was doing.

"Thanks," Marisa replied.

Marisa stopped short of saying anymore as it would have made no difference. She was tired and needed to think. With that she was dropped off at the door of the hotel and Peter and Julie went back to the life they knew. Marisa realized that she had no idea what life would be like with a real job and a family. Marisa walked up to the door of the main lobby, it was close to five o'clock in the morning and the door was locked.

Marisa peered through the front door window. There was a doorman sitting in a chair sleeping. Marisa knocked. "Hey let me in, I need to use your phone!"

The doorman woke up and shook his head no. As he did, Marisa stepped back. She could see herself in the glass of the hotels front window. Her hair was matted, her clothes were torn and the sports bra looked like it had never been washed. Suddenly she felt embarrassed. She had never seen herself in such disarray. She was not used to being so down and without the luxuries of the life her drug money bought. She turned around and sat on the curb. Tired, alone, desperate, and too close to New York, too close to where they would be looking for her, she was coming unglued.

Holding her head in her hands, Marisa heard a voice from behind. "Hey, I can't let you in but here is my cell phone. Use it and give it back. Now don't steal it. It is a prepaid cell but I want it back."

Marisa turned to see the doorman looking out of the side door. "Thank you so much. I will use it right here and give it back."

Marisa took the phone and dialed the only person she could trust.

•   •   •

Jan was sitting at her home office desk, staring blankly out the window when the phone rang. It took about four rings before Jan decided to answer. She knew it would be Marisa. "Hello?"

"Jan, this is Marisa."

"Marisa, where are you?"

"Can I talk on this phone Jan?"

"I think it is still okay. They may bug my phone but I doubt they will be able to get a wiretap order from a judge until later in the morning for my phone. Have you lost your mind? You know that the government will never help you now that you have escaped."

"I had no choice. The Feds wanted William and he would give them Damian to help me. If he had any hope of getting a cooperation deal that would let him out of prison before he was an old man, he would have to cooperate against Damian. That would have gotten him killed, though I think he is already dead. I was in love, I didn't want William to go to jail. I am the reason he is dead."

"How do you know William is dead?" Jan asked.

"Damian killed him and nearly killed me as well." Marisa began to sob. For the first time she realized what a mess she was in and that she had lost the only person in her family she cared about.

"I am so sorry Marisa. Why would Damian kill William and try to kill you? I thought he loved you and was your brother's friend."

Through her sobs, Marisa said, "I guess he can't afford the risk of me breaking down in prison and exposing what I know. I think he killed William because he was careless and knew he would cooperate if arrested. Damian will do anything to avoid being identified or go to jail."

"How did you escape?"

"I will tell you all about it when I see you. Jan, I have no place to go. I need to come to your house. I need time to think, get cleaned up and figure out what to do."

"Marisa that will not be safe, the government will be watching me and looking for you here. It would be illegal for me to harbor or help a fugitive."

"I know. I figure we have one or two days before they realize I am out of

New York and not dead. Damian tried to kill me by blowing up the boat we used as part of the escape plan. We both jumped overboard before the explosion. I do not think Damian thought I would get away. The Feds will be looking for me closer to New York and New Jersey and will concentrate on the airports and roads. I need some money wired to an account where I am right now in the name of Christina Benson." Marisa gave Jan the address of the quaint hotel she was sitting outside of. She could only hope the doorman would help her even more by letting her in and allowing money to be wired to the hotel

Jan was conflicted about helping Marisa as this could be seen as helping an escaped convict. She could lose her law license if she helped Marisa in the wrong way. She could try and talk her into turning herself in over the phone she thought but that was unlikely to be effective. She wanted to help Marisa but she knew she would have to turn her in herself once she got to Atlanta. For a moment she hesitated but she remembered Kellie's sister's death, if only someone had helped her in the moment or she reached out before taking those pills she might have lived. It was not the same with Marisa but if Jan could reach her and get her turned in, the outcome of these events might be mitigated. Right now, with the escape, Marisa was looking at even more time if she was caught.

"I will get someone to send you the money but not me. Don't call again. If you come here all I am going to do is try and convince you to turn yourself in, which you should do now."

With that, Jan hung up and contemplated how to pull this off without getting in trouble herself. She had to convince Marisa to turn herself in.

Marisa knocked on the window to get the doorman to come to her. "Thanks for the phone." Marisa handed it back to the doorman. Just before letting it go she asked one more favor.

"I am getting some money wired to this hotel, could you get it for me? I will give you ten percent of whatever amount is wired."

"Ten percent you say?"

"The money should get here by noon if it is wired first thing this morning," Marisa replied.

Feeling sorry for Marisa and the possibility of some fast cash the doorman offered his help. "I tell you what; there is a cot in the basement area where the linens are washed. Sleep there for a few hours and I will see what I can do. My name is Dan and I want twenty percent."

"Ok, done! You will never know how much I appreciate this. I am down on my luck, my boyfriend kicked me out of the apartment last night and I have been wandering the streets all night trying to think of something to do. My friend will send me some money so I can get out of here. My name is Christina."

"You look pretty disheveled but I understand, I have been there myself. Come on, I will sneak you in."

• • •

"Was that Marisa on the phone babe ?" asked Kellie.

"Yes," replied Jan.

"Honey, I know you are going to help her but you are putting yourself and your career on the line."

"I am trying not to. I can help her as long as I try and convince her to turn herself in. I admit it is a gray area and risky. Kellie, who can help me get her some money without being traced?"

"I really do not want any part of this but I know you will do whatever it takes to help Marisa regardless of what I say. I know I can't talk you out of it. Something about this case has touched a rescue nerve in you. I know a private investigator from my FBI years. We did surveillance on him for years but could never catch him doing anything criminal though we knew he had likely helped a lot of guys we arrested. I never used him, but his reputation is that he can get things done no one else wants to do. I kept his information when I left the FBI just in case."

Kellie handed Jan a card with only a number on it, no name. "Don't ask him his name; just tell him what you want. He is really good at staying under the radar."

"Thanks baby, I love you. I know this is hard for you since you were an FBI agent. Sometimes there are people in this world who do something terribly wrong, who are really good people and deserve a break. Marisa is that type of person even though she is not helping herself by escaping. Poverty and love can make you do stupid things."

"I know your heart, Jan; you see good in almost everyone. I only hope your faith in Marisa is not misplaced."

With that Kellie left Jan to her thoughts and continued to pack for Colombia. Ranger laid down at Jan's feet, he could sense her distress.

•　　•　　•

Marisa woke to Dan shaking her lightly.

"Time to get up sleeping beauty, it is around eight thirty in the morning. I got you some clothes to wear and a breakfast buffet pass but I have to get you out of here, so when you get upstairs act like a guest."

Marisa turned over slowly and in great agony. Every muscle in her body screamed at her for having such a rough night. She pushed her body to escape from a federal prison only to jump from a moving aircraft, swim in cold water, endure emotional devastation and think on her feet for hours. She was sore, had a headache and a sore throat from being in wet clothes most of the night.

Dan's six foot, well-shaped frame stood over Marisa. "Dan, you are an angel. Thank you. How can I repay you?"

"I don't know what is going on in your life, but if you get things sorted out and you get back to New Jersey look me up. You are beautiful, worth a shot right?" he said with a teasing smile.

"I look like crap. You need to get on the day shift, the night shift has you seeing things."

Marisa noticed he wasn't bad looking. He was young and fit. He was genuinely trying to be a nice guy. He had a light brown skin , black short hair and light brown eyes. He spoke to her in a soft voice seeming to be sympathetic to her plight.

"I don't know why you've helped me, but I will never forget you," she said.

"Here are some clothes and soap. You can wash up in the laundry room sink. As soon as you have changed go on up to the breakfast buffet, eat and enjoy. I will find you as soon as the money comes in. I am off at eleven and can join you for coffee."

Dan handed the free breakfast card to Marisa and left.

"How will you get the money from the hotel if I'm not a guest?"

"I told them you were my girlfriend and that family was sending you some money for a trip home. Pretty good huh?"

"Pure genius! It should come in the name of Christina Benson."

"Is that your real name?" asked Dan.

Marisa never replied; she just smiled politely.

•   •   •

William found himself lying on his back floating, staring at a black sky. At first he thought he had died and was an angel flying in heavenly waters. He heard muffled sounds but could not tell where he was. The last thing he remembered was flying through the air in a ball of flames. As he began to orient himself, he felt a burning pain in his back and legs. They burned but were not on fire. He was chilled to the bone. He was confused as to what had happened to him. Surely he was dead. This must be hell, not heaven, he thought, cold as ice but burning at the same time. William could see the sky; what a cruel joke, he thought to himself. This was his penance for a life of crime, he would spend the rest of his days in pain and cold for his past sins, always seeing heaven but never getting there. His confusing thoughts were overwhelming. He could hardly breathe. He struggled to grasp his situation.

William slowly began to move his head in an attempt to look around. His mind was foggy, but in the distance he could see some type of platform. It must be a mirage, a way out of hell, but unreachable. He tried to move and realized he was in real water, cold and dark. Swim, he told himself, swim. As he began to move, he could only feel excruciating pain. He could not move his left arm.

Gradually, he started to swim on his side with one arm, using it like a paddle, and frog kicking his legs which were also in pain. He could see he was making progress moving closer to the platform he could see in the early morning light. When he got near the platform he could see it was some type of dock on a shoreline. As he approached he could see people fishing. He tried to call out for help but he could not hear the sound of his own voice.

"Help me, I think I'm hurt," William struggled to say. His mind heard the words he thought he was speaking but he could not hear himself.

Someone was talking to him but he could only see their mouths moving. He stared blankly at this person he could see but not hear standing on the dock above him.

"Hey buddy, you okay. Hey, can you hear me?" Kamal tried asking the man in the water.

"Hey! You alright? He looks bad," Kamal said to someone William could see standing next to him. . "Man Joey this dudes clothes are burned and his arm is just hanging there."

"I can see it, Kamal." Joey replied. "I'll call an ambulance on my cell phone."

The man in the water finally seemed to hear them and cried out—"No!"

"Buddy you are a mess, you need help."

At that, the man passed out.

•   •   •

Marisa was stuffing her face with food from the breakfast buffet. She was wearing an "I Love New York" tee shirt and a pair of oversized jeans. She looked like a tourist trying to look hip without being classy. She was so hungry she was afraid someone would think she was a pig. She piled her first two plates so high she thought she would drop the food on the floor walking back to her table. The coffee was so good she drank three cups before she even started eating, nothing in the prison could compare to this moment. Marisa vowed never to forget the little things in life and how important they are, including her freedom.

"Hi, Christina. I see you're enjoying your meal." Dan had seen her eating, watching her for a few minutes, decided to join her.

"This is the best meal I have ever had. Thank you so much for the pass."

"If I did not know any better I would think you have been eating out of a garbage can. The way you are shoveling it down, it looks like you haven't eaten in a week."

Marisa had to be careful what she said. Dan was more right than she cared to admit.

"Being thrown out of your apartment, without clothes or money is pretty bad," Marisa said.

"I was never thrown out, but my girlfriend left me for someone else not too long ago. Hurts, don't it?"

Dan got up to get himself a cup of coffee and a donut and check the front desk for the money. Marisa stared at him as he walked away. She longed for a regular life but this was not it.

When Dan came back he handed her an envelope.

"I think this is your money. It was at the front desk."

Marisa opened the envelope that had the name Christina Benson on the front. Inside were twenty one hundred dollar bills. Two thousand dollars was more than she had hoped for. This would get her out of New Jersey quick and be enough for it to have been worth Dan's help.

"Dan, I will give you an extra hundred dollars if you take me to the bus station."

Marisa knew she had to get as far away from where she was as possible before traveling south. She decided to risk a cheap bus ticket to Atlanta.

"I'm off now and have nothing to do but go home and sleep. Hell, I can sleep when I'm dead. Sure, I'll take you anywhere you want to go but no need to give me any more money, just your phone number will do."

Marisa knew she could not give him her phone number. "Dan, let me get yours so that I can call you when I come back here."

"Ok, I hope you will call me some day."

Dan gave Marisa a napkin with his phone number on it. Marisa stuck the napkin in the back pocket of her empty jeans along with the remaining cash.

•   •   •

Jan was sitting at her computer reviewing transcripts. She was reading the same line over and over again, unable to concentrate. Kellie had left to catch her noon flight to Colombia. Jan was alone with her thoughts and of course the ever vigilant Ranger. Ranger always knew when something was wrong, but all he could do was offer quiet support lying near Jan's feet.

"Ranger, I only hope that the number Kellie gave me, and the message I left the investigator gets the job done." Jan was talking to Ranger and to herself at the same time. "It seems strange that the voice message called it 'The Charity,' but it fits and hopefully won't connect me with helping Marisa." Ranger just looked up at Jan who responded with pets between his ears.

Kellie told Jan that a lot of ex-law enforcement people used this discrete investigator. Payment was sent to a P.O. Box in cash only. No names, no receipts. The post office box was frequently changed and only a few knew when and where it was reopened by a simple card in the mail with that information on it. No return address or stamp and no internet contact. This person was totally off the grid.

• • •

William woke up in some kind of hospital bed. He was groggy but knew he was alive and no longer dreaming. He sat up slowly, hot pain running through his body. As he looked around he could see he was in a room made up to look more like a hospital room than someone's bedroom. There was a defibrillator in the room and a tray with what looked like hospital operating room instruments. A lot of bandages and towels were on a dresser in the corner. There were no mirrors or decorations in the room and the floor was bare.

"Good morning. Feeling better?"

William stared at a woman standing in the doorway who did not look like a nurse but was acting like one. "Where am I?" he asked.

"Kamal brought you here. I'm a nurse and I also privately treat neighbors and friends in special circumstances."

"What does that mean? There is all this hospital equipment in here."

"Well, when things get out of hand in the neighborhood that are not too serious and people don't want the police or doctors to ask questions, they come to me. I'm pretty good at stitching people up who might have minor wounds or injuries. I should have been a doctor but ran out of money and time."

William looked at his body. His left arm was in a sling and he was in an open hospital gown with gauze wrapped around his legs. He could feel a dull burning in his legs, left arm and lower back. He looked like he had been wounded in war.

"What happened to me?"

"We have no idea. Kamal and Joey were fishing at Owls Head Park when you washed up and they brought you here to me. They said something about you mumbling not to take you in an ambulance to a hospital. They figured I was the only option considering the shape you were in."

"I'm grateful. How bad am I?"

"You have some bad bruising and first degree burns on your left arm and you have some first and second degree burns on your lower back and legs. Looks to me you are lucky to be alive. The helmet, life vest and flight jacket you were wearing were badly burned but saved you from more serious injury, at least on your back. Oh yeah, despite the helmet, your hair was burned in patches so we shaved your head. Hope you don't mind. Everything else appears okay. I gave you a strong sedative and some pain killers to help with the pain and a salve that has to be put on the second degree burns twice a day with new dressing. . Nothing worse than burns, they're the injury that just keeps on giving."

"What is your name?" William asked as he winced in pain trying to sit up.

"My name, for your purpose, is Rosalyn; you can call me Rosey, that is R O S E Y not I E. That's what I like. You rest now John, someone will come back soon with something to eat. I know you must be hungry."

"That I am, but how do you know my name?"

"In what was left of your leather jacket we found a license with the name John Ramos on it and your picture, figured that was you."

Rosey left the room. As the fog of waking up began to put life back in his mind and body, William started to remember some of what happened. The license was one of the false identification document's Damian seemed to be able to manufacture at will. He remembered getting it from Damian in case he got caught picking up Marisa on the prison roof. Damian had wallet size pictures of all his crew just for this purpose. He was always changing the off-loaders names and identities in case they got caught.

William remembered flying to the prison and picking up Marisa and then flying the Ultralite out into the bay, but everything after that was foggy. The next thing he recalled was an explosion that propelled him into the air. He was on fire. Then he seemed to fall forever before hitting a brick wall. He had no memory of anything else. He thought about Marisa and wondered if she was dead, though he remembered she jumped from the Ultralite helicopter before the explosion. It pained him to think he was the cause of his sister's death. He had no doubts that Damian tried to kill him but he was not sure about Marisa.

•   •   •

Dan took Marisa to the bus station in Newark. She had no idea how much effort the authorities were putting into finding her, but she had to risk getting out of the New York and New Jersey area fast. The only way to do that was by Greyhound express. It would take twenty-four hours to get to Atlanta from Newark. Even though it was called express, there were still stops along the way for other passengers. The trip would be longer than she wanted, but it was the best of all the options. With all the security at the airports it would be too risky to fly. The only identification she had on her was the picture ID from the prison. She would have to try and flash that for the bus ticket and hope no one looks at it closely.

On the way to the bus station, Marisa had Dan stop at a Target store to buy some roll-on luggage, toiletries, underwear, another more fitting pair of jeans, a sun hat, sunglasses and a couple of t-shirts. Marisa's slender body could fit into something a little less bulky than what Dan had found for her. Having lost weight in prison, Marisa's body was thin and pale. Marisa bought a wallet at the Target with a window slip to put her prison ID in hoping it would make it look more official. She stuffed some other official looking papers, a receipt and some coupons, in the wallet along with her money hoping this would make her look more legitimate.

On the way to the station Dan told her his story. How he had loved one girl since he was in the sixth grade and she sat next to him. He was certain he would marry her. They dated for five years after high school and just when he was going to pop the question she said goodbye. She found another, older doctor set with money. Dan could not compete with that.

"Someday I will settle down with a family. I'm finishing school, working on my degree in psychology. I want to help troubled teens, or teach in a public high school. Tough job but seems to be worthwhile," he told Marisa.

"Noble to say the least." Marisa thought to herself that she was one of those troubled youths and wished someone had saved her from this life she now was running back into.

"I admit it sounds corny and uncool, but it really is where my heart lies."

"No, I really admire your determination. At least it is an honest living."

Marisa caught herself and withdrew from the conversation. The last thing she needed to do was trust someone with her pathetic life story and what she had done.

They arrived at the bus terminal around two in the afternoon.

"Daniel Howard, future teacher of the masses, I will never forget you."

Maybe we will see each other again," he said. "Look Christina, I know you are in some kind of trouble. If you need me, call the number I gave you. I mean it, call me."

"I will Dan, you have done enough, more than I expected. You did not even know me but helped me anyway, that says volumes about who you are as a person."

Marisa handed him an additional two hundred dollars but he refused to take more than his share which she had already given him. It was hard for Marisa to turn away and leave. He had been so kind, and besides her lawyer, he was the first decent person she had met in her life that wasn't dealing in drugs, laundering drug money or living an inflated dishonest lifestyle.

Marisa went into the terminal and looked for the first bus route to Atlanta. There were police around and at least one drug dog she could see walking around checking luggage but they did not seem to be interested in her. She went to the window with her sun hat and glasses on to purchase her bus ticket to Atlanta.

• • •

William was trying to get up and on his feet. He needed to get out of New York. As he rose to his feet, and tried to stand, he could feel the pain in his legs from the burns. With great discomfort, he stood up, holding onto the bed for leverage; he immediately bent over and threw up.

"Easy dog, you've been badly injured," came a voice from the doorway.

William felt a cool compress on the back of his neck. As he looked up he saw two guys, one black, and one white. "Who are you?" he asked.

"I'm Kamal and this is my friend Joey. We found you at Owls Head Park. Man, you were really messed up."

"Thank you for not taking me to the hospital." William felt like someone was holding a hot iron on his legs and back. He could barely move.

"I need to get out of here," William said.

"Anytime you want man," replied Joey somewhat sarcastically. "We're not holding you hostage."

"I'm sorry, I don't mean to sound ungrateful but I'm in a bit of trouble and need to leave."

"Everyone has a story dude," replied Kamal. "What can we do to help?"

"Take me to the airport."

"Consider it done, John," Kamal said. "We found some identification in your wallet with about three grand in hundred dollar bills in a sealed plastic bag in your pants. You flush man. You rob somebody or something?"

William could not reply. His story was too complicated, and he did not want to involve the people who helped him and saved his life. The money was for the escape once he ditched the Ultralite.

It took William some time to steady himself. Rosey came in, and gave Kamal and Joey the wave of her hand to get out.

"John Ramos," Rosey said, "you can't go anywhere for at least two or three days. I need to put the burn cream on your injuries at least twice a day and change the bandages for at least two more days to avoid you getting an infection."

Rosey told Kamal and Joey to get some of their clothes for John and to not bother him or take him anywhere.

"Sorry John, we have to do what Rosey says, she's the boss," declared Joey.

"I have to leave here. I can't tell you why. How can I repay you, and get out of here?" William said.

"I am not sure what trouble you are in but there is no need to pay me," Rosey said. "I do this all the time. I can't make you stay but if you go you have to change those bandages and be careful."

Kamal handed William his wallet as if to say, give the lady some money. William handed Rosey seven single one hundred dollar bills. After a little polite protest, she accepted the money. Rosey could see William was not going anywhere just yet.

William was tired and drained from just standing up. He had to go back to bed. His trip to Atlanta would have to wait.

•   •   •

Marisa was able to get her bus ticket to Atlanta without even having to show her ID and sat in the middle of the bus by a window. This was always her backup plan with William. If things went south on any level they would meet at her attorney's office in Atlanta, as far away as possible from New York. Her mind wandered through her experiences in the last twenty-four hours. So much had happened, so much gone wrong. She hated Damian for killing William and trying to kill her. Marisa knew more than he thought she did. She knew how to find him, or she could turn herself in and destroy him. The second option was what Jan would try to convince her to do. It was not Marisa's choice for now but she had to get to Jan for advice. Her heart sank, aware that William would never join her.

As the bus pulled away Marisa saw the front page of the local paper in the distribution sales box, "Prison Inmate Makes Daring Rooftop Escape!" She could only hope no one on the bus saw the paper and recognized her. Her prison photo was the lead frame before the article. She sunk lower in her seat, pulling the sunhat down over her forehead and pretended she was sleeping.

On the long ride Marisa had time to think about what she could do to change the future. She felt great despair knowing her only choices were to either leave the country or turn herself in. She did not want to spend the rest of her life in prison or always looking over her shoulder if she ran. There had to be another way.

•   •   •

Damian took a private jet to Atlanta and was already sitting outside Jan's law office waiting for her to leave. He and Caleb had been up all night with the escape plans, but were able to get some sleep on the two hour flight to Atlanta. He would wait for the right moment. The last few days of preparation and problems were more than Damian wanted. He had hoped he would be on his way to Colombia by now to update the Vasquez family on the termination of William and Marisa and report that he had good information on other informants so he could be instructed to terminate them as well. He did not want someone else to get to the family first with the wrong story of what had happened.

Damian was mad at himself for missing his opportunity to kill Marisa; then he could have let her attorney live. The body count was getting a bit high even for Damian. He had to leave no trace of Marisa or Jan and it would be too hard to do that in the States. If he killed them here, there would be a lot of heat on the entire organization, and he had no idea what Marisa has told the government so far that could lead them to him. The Vasquez family did not need to know everything, just the results and that their confidence in his abilities should not change.

"Caleb, have the Gulfstream jet standing by at Peachtree DeKalb Airport. We need it to be ready to leave on a moment's notice."

"We will be ready, Damian. We will have to stop in Texas to refuel on our way to Colombia. We should be able to do it without detection if we can make it in one day and stop at the Big Springs airport. We have a connection in customs there. For enough money we will not have to go through the usual customs searches."

•   •   •

Jan decided to go to her law office after not hearing from Marisa again. She arrived at around at eight a.m. Monday morning, coffee in hand, Ranger at her side. She often took Ranger to the office for company and security.

When David came in at nine, Jan had been pacing the floor of her office trying to figure out what to do and what not to do to help Marisa. Jan had already updated David by phone on his way in about the call from the prison.

"Jan, have you heard from Kellie since she left?" David asked.

"Not that I know of but I need to check my e-mail. I need to keep busy today David, so pile it on."

"No problem, we have several pretrial motions to get done on a new matter and an appeal to get started on."

David was good at keeping Jan organized and busy. Today she needed to keep busy as her mind was swirling with what to do and where Marisa was.

•   •   •

Marisa sat staring out the bus window. She had slept fitfully though she was still dog tired and sore. The bus may have been less conspicuous, but the ride was hell. All Marisa could think about was William's death and Damian's betrayal. She knew she could not go back to jail. She remembered how much she loved Damian, allowed herself to be blinded by what he offered, all that she had never had. They traveled together to so many beautiful places, Rome, Paris, and Saint-Tropez on the coast of southern France, his favorite romantic getaway. He loved to be among the rich and famous. He would tell everyone he was in his family's oil and gas business, from old money in Texas. His drug money made him feel important, mingling with movie stars and entrepreneurs.

Marisa had been romanced by the easy money and his exotic lifestyle. It was easy to forget the risks and fear of being caught every time she worked an off-load job when she was with Damian. It was so much money, there was nothing Damian would not do for her and she could not do for herself. He was attentive, loving, and made her feel special. When they went out to exotic international restaurants he wore tailored suits and looked like he owned the world. He kept in shape and loved having a beautiful woman on his arm. Marisa thought she was that women, and would be forever, but she realized now she was blinded by greed and love. She never realized until now that Damian let everyone else take the risks while he reaped the rewards. He really was manipulative and cared for no one but his precious drug business and false image. Nothing, Marisa thought now, was worth her freedom or her life, not even Damian. There had to be a way out.

• • •

Jan was not able to concentrate any longer. It was six o'clock on Monday night and David was still at the office with her though she had tried to send him home.

"David, let's get out of here," Jan declared. "I need some air. Thanks for staying."

"No problem. Maybe Marisa will call tonight."

Jan drove home with the top down. It was a clear September evening with low humidity and a hint of the coming fall in the air. With the radio blaring Florence and The Machine, she had no idea Damian and his bodyguard were following her home.

• • •

"Wake up Damian!" Caleb shouted. "They are leaving the office and Marisa never showed up!"

Damian had been dosing. When he heard Caleb's voice he sat up and watched as Jan said goodbye to her assistant in front of the office and got in her Lexus convertible with her large German Sheppard curled up on the passenger seat.

• • •

Jan opened the front door of their midtown home, and she and Ranger, tail wagging, stepped inside. The first thing Ranger did was check the house for Kellie. "Sorry boy, she is gone for a while; it is just you and me."

Jan called Ranger and he obediently came back to her side. As usual he started barking to let Jan know he was ready for supper. This was a soft bark more like a whine, very different than if he was reacting to danger. He was a good dog, smart and spoiled. "All right boy let's both have something to eat." Jan also poured a glass of wine from the second bottle she and Kellie had opened the night before.

• • •

"Caleb, I want you to case the house. We need to grab the lawyer so Marisa will not give us a hard time if she shows up. Marisa won't let anything happen to her attorney friend, so even if Marisa does not show up we can use the attorney to get her to come to us. We get the lawyer, and Marisa will come quietly either way."

With that, Caleb went up to the front of the house. The front door was mostly window but you could see inside, though a little blurred from a sheer curtain that covered the window. . He immediately heard the ominous bark of a big dog. He looked inside and could see Jan from a narrow view through the hall to the kitchen. Jan was looking through the mail on the kitchen counter drinking a glass of wine. He could not see the dog, but he could hear it.

• • •

Jan had let Ranger out into the backyard after he ate, and she heard him start barking loudly. She knew it was not his usual conversation bark with neighboring dogs or signal to let him back in the house. He was upset, pacing back and forth on the deck in front of the French doors, barking loudly.

"What's up boy?" She could see he was agitated. She let him in, and he immediately bolted for the front door. He was barking even louder now so Jan went to investigate.

Caleb saw the German Sheppard coming to the front door and ducked. He crawled away and hid behind some bushes on the opposite side of the neighbor's house.

"Easy Ranger, sit, good boy."

Jan could see Ranger was not in the mood to sit. He was very agitated. She peered out the front window behind the living room couch. Not seeing anything, she held Ranger's collar so he would not bolt out the front door and opened it slightly. Jan was never worried when Ranger was around, no one would dare come in on her. She did, however, want to be sure no one was around. Ranger was still upset and barking but Jan could not see anything. She shut the door and went back inside.

"Quiet Ranger, hush, sit, down." Ranger followed Jan's commands though reluctantly especially when she commanded him to lie down and motioned with her hand to do so. He never took his eyes off the front door. He did as Jan commanded but went to the hallway, where he could see the front door, to lie down not wanting to leave his strategic position if any danger approached.

•   •   •

"That German Sheppard is huge! We can never get past the dog!" Caleb exclaimed as he returned to the car out of breath.

"Be patient my friend. We will get her. It is going to be another long night so go get us some food and come back with plenty of coffee for you." Damian laughed as he said this knowing he would be able to get some sleep while Caleb kept watch.

•   •   •

William had not slept much so he decided to try and get out of the bed and move around. As he started to get up he noticed some sweat suit clothes on the chair beside his bed and put them on. The loose fit helped him move slowly without rubbing on his injuries. There were slippers on the floor as well and he slipped into them. With pain pills in hand he walked gingerly to the kitchen table. It was seven in the morning on Tuesday, and Rosey was already up and getting ready for work.

"Coffee, John?"

"Thanks, Rosey. I need to leave today. Do I have your permission?" William asked sheepishly.

"I can't stop you, but another day of rest would be better for you. I know you got trouble and you need to attend to it. Kamal and Joey will take you wherever you want to go."

"Rosey, I can never thank you enough for what you have done. "

"No thanks necessary. Take care of yourself."

With that Rosey was out the door.

"You know John, Rosey is special," Joey said as he walked into the kitchen. "She is used to people in trouble coming and going without knowing why. This way, if the law came around, or others with bad intentions, she would not have to lie. The cops always come to Rosey when there is trouble in the neighborhood, but they also know she never asks a lot of questions and could seldom provide them any significant information."

"What does she do?" William asked.

"She is a nurse and has treated burns, minor flesh wounds from gunshots, stitched up knife cuts, set broken bones, and iced bruises. She always keeps supplies in the house she gets from the hospital she works at. The pain meds are from the street. There is always someone selling in the neighborhood.

Rosey had given William a bottle of Oxycodone with 25 pills to take as needed for the pain. William was drinking his coffee when Kamal came in.

"Man, you look a lot better," said Kamal.

"Thanks to some rest and pain pills, but I need to go to the Newark airport."

"Can you walk?" asked Joey.

"I have to manage. The burns are painful but my arm feels okay. Besides the pain meds really work."

Kamal and Joey gave William some loose street clothes to change into and some extra personal items and t-shirts in a small backpack for the trip. On the way to the airport they told him how they came to be under Rosey's wing.

"Rosey is a good woman," Kamal said. "She takes in foster children and helps people in trouble. She is always trying to change the way people think about doing bad stuff that can get them in trouble, helping them get a fresh start. She is not confident that the justice system is fair to the poor and under-privileged, not a system that tries to help, just incarcerate, so she does a little rehabilitation of her own if you know what I mean. Joey and I are both the result of drug addicted parents who never recovered. She took us in and made us better people when no one else would risk adopting two older kids. We are both headed for college this year thanks to Rosey and her efforts in helping us get grants. She works as a nurse supervisor for a local hospital. We are not allowed to tell anyone where she works. She put herself through college when her mother abandoned her at her grandmother's house."

"Your secrets are safe with me." William wished he had put the same effort into his own life instead of following Damian. Here he was now physically and emotionally messed up. Someone tried to kill him, someone he thought he could trust and was his friend.

When Joey and Kamal let him off at the airport, William gave them two hundred dollars each. "Consider it part of your college fund," he said. He thanked them again and gingerly walked inside the terminal. He needed a round trip ticket to Atlanta. Damian had taught him to always buy a round trip ticket even if you were not going to return to your city of departure. This kept the airport cops from becoming too suspicious. He knew he had to purchase the ticket in cash which might arouse some suspicion, but he did not have any fake credit cards, only the fake identification. He was not planning to ever come back to New York.

William walked slowly up to the Delta ticket counter to buy his ticket. "I need a round trip ticket to Atlanta."

The ticket agent looked at him with some compassion; he could see the pain in William's face whenever he moved. "What happened to you?" the agent asked.

"I had a car accident." He did not want to tell her he was burned but she could see some of the damage from his scalp. When the hair came back in it would cover the red spots. At least there were no second degree burns on his head or face. He thought about wearing a hat but knew he would have to take it off for security and wearing it rubbed on his burns. Thank God he had a helmet on when the Ultralite blew up.

"I have a four o'clock flight that is open."

"That will be fine." The ticket cost six hundred and eighty-seven dollars with tax. Always a rip off when you fly on the day you purchase the ticket. William handed her the cash.

"Sir, can I see some identification please?"

William handed the ticket agent the false identification Damian had prepared for him. The ticket agent looked at it and at him with some suspicion.

"Not a good likeness without your hair."

That concerned William as he had not thought about how he must look compared to his picture.

"Well it is me, at least when I was handsome." He tried to be humorous to distract from any suspicions.

At that the agent asked: "Will you need some assistance to the gate? I can get a wheelchair if you like."

William knew it would be easier to get a ride in the wheelchair. His legs were stiff, and it hurt when his pants legs rubbed against the bandages.

"Yes, thank you, that would be nice," he said.

When the wheelchair arrived, he got in. At security, the wheelchair worked. He got a lot of sympathetic looks from the TSA workers and even though they checked his identification twice, he walked through the x-ray machine gingerly without incident after taking his shoes off and putting his bag on the x-ray belt.

As he was being wheeled down the hall to his gate, he saw the newspaper dispenser. Front page news, "Inmate Escapes from Rooftop of Federal Prison." Marisa's picture was all over the New York papers. He popped another pain pill before getting on the plane to Atlanta.

• • •

William's flight was slightly delayed but landed around seven forty-five Tuesday evening, two days after their harrowing escape and his near-death experience. He had no idea where Marisa would be, but he was certain she would find her way to Atlanta. They had talked about it before; if trouble came, and they were separated, they would meet in Atlanta and go to her lawyer's office. This way they would be together and near an attorney they trusted. Though Jan was retained after Marisa got arrested, they knew about her reputation. They researched several federal attorneys always anticipating the day it would all come crashing down. They never thought it would but felt better knowing someone would be there to help if it did.

William immediately got off the plane and dialed Jan's office number. Her answering service would pick up until ten p.m. and then it would be voice mail. He needed to talk to a person. William let the phone ring until the service picked up.

"Law office of Jan Bergin and associates, can we help you?"

"I need to speak to Ms. Bergin."

"She is not in. I can take a message and see that she gets it."

William left an urgent message using his alias. He did not trust the service and could not risk telling them who he was. His message simply told Jan to call John Ramos at the Marriott Courtyard in downtown Atlanta as soon as she got the message and that it was about her client Marisa.

William was tired from the exertion of the trip. He caught a cab at the airport and headed for the hotel. He would get some food and go to sleep; he was exhausted and in pain. He would try Jan again in the morning.

• • •

"Hi babe, made it to Colombia. I miss you already. The flight was long but I got a lot of work done. Sending you this e-mail from the Inter-Continental Hotel in Medellin but am headed out to the countryside for a few days so will have limited communication options. We are headed to Turbo and Apartado tomorrow. Rough areas but we will have our translator and bodyguards. Not to worry, though I know you will. Love, Kellie."

Jan read Kellie's e-mail and sent her one back. She did not mention anything about Marisa. "Stay safe, we love you." She put a smiley face on the e-mail and found an emoji of a dog paw.

"Come on Ranger, it's late; let's go to bed." Jan and Ranger went up-stairs but she left a light on downstairs as she always did when Kellie was gone. Sleeping alone never felt as secure as when Kellie was spooned up next to her. Sleep was not easy to find; things didn't feel right. Even Ranger was not himself and laid on the bed, eyes open, ears twitching. Jan could feel his uneasiness.

Jan decided to get up at five a.m., since she could not sleep, and just get on with her day. She still had not heard from Marisa. As she walked out of the house to her car she could feel Ranger getting uneasy. His ears were up, nose in the air and he was pulling on his leash instead of standing by Jan's side.

"What's up boy?" she said to Ranger. Even though Jan looked around she could not see anything unusual. "Come on Ranger, let's go." Ranger dutifully followed Jan to her car. Jan had no idea she was being followed.

•   •   •

"David did you get any messages on the voice mail or the answering service?" Jan asked when she got to the office.

"As a matter of fact I did. There was a message from the answering service from someone named John Ramos. Do you know anyone by that name? He is not on our client list."

"No does not sound familiar. Did he say what it was about?"

"Yes, said it was about your client Marisa," replied David.

"Well, I have no idea who that is. It could be someone looking for her after her escape; so I am reluctant to return the call."

•   •   •

It was around 6 p.m. on Tuesday when the bus from New Jersey pulled into the station in downtown Atlanta. Marisa was even more tired and sore from the long bus ride. The bus made so many stops that she wondered how the bus service could call the trip an express run. They switched drivers somewhere in Kentucky, but Marisa was in and out trying to sleep and could not tell where they were at any given time. She had never been so uncomfortable trying to sleep. There is no way to rest on a bus. She felt grimy, needing a shower and something other than fast food and vending machine snacks to eat. No chance of either, she could not risk being seen in public even if she was hundreds of miles from New York. The Federal Marshals have a long reach and likely have sent out a most wanted alert to all federal jurisdictions.

When Marisa got off the bus with the other weary travelers, someone from the bus came up behind her. She was groggy and not expecting anyone to speak to her.

"Miss, you left your paper on the seat. Did you want it? I want to make sure you wanted to throw it away." It was the bus driver.

Marisa purchased a New York paper in a bus terminal somewhere in Pennsylvania during a bus refueling stop. She read the article about her escape. The paper made her sound like a modern day Al Capone. "Dangerous female drug queen mastermind's rooftop prison escape . . . considered armed and dangerous . . . call police or FBI . . ."—the article went on with fill in, lacking details from the police accounts of the incident. Most of the article discussed the lack of Bureau of Prisons security and how someone could have escaped by helicopter.

"Thank you. I think I will take it." Marisa said.

"I read the paper myself on one of our stops. Did you see the story about the prison escape? Man that was something. You look a lot like the girl in the picture, only your hair is longer."

Marisa froze; she had taken off her hat and sunglasses a long time ago. There were bus terminal security police and drug dogs always nearby. Could they be aware of her? She started to stutter.

"Uh, well, uh, I don't think so."

The picture was from the mug shot on the day of her arrest. She had short hair then. She was glad she let her hair grow over the past eighteen months while in prison.

"Sure does have a resemblance," said the driver. He looked at her for a moment longer, handed her the paper and left.

Marisa had to get out of there, clean up, food would have to wait.

• • •

Jan tossed and turned all night again Tuesday night after hearing nothing from Marisa all day. She was restless with thoughts of Marisa, Kellie, and work. An endless stream of thoughts she could do nothing about. This time she woke up even earlier than the day before. It was four in the morning on Wednesday. After a cup of coffee and a quick check of her e-mails and Facebook, Jan called the office and left David a message that she would be working at home in hopes of hearing from Marisa.

When she asked Ranger if he wanted to go for a walk, he was up and sprinting to the door with his leash in his mouth. He knew where his leash hung and how to get it. Damian and Caleb watched Jan leave with the dog from the car they had been sitting in since arriving in Atlanta late Monday.

"Damian," Caleb said, "I am tired of waiting, we need to move on this."

"Patience Caleb, our time is coming. Today we will either take Jan or if Marisa shows up, both of them. If we get Jan today we will get Marisa eventually. I will take action today no matter what."

• • •

The streets were quiet, even for Midtown Atlanta. There were a couple of early runners but not much by way of traffic. Jan never noticed the deep blue Jeep Cherokee with darkened back windows across the street. It looked like any other car that would be in their neighborhood.

After walking for two miles around the neighborhood Jan returned home. She let Ranger out in the backyard but left the door open so he could get back in. It looked like a heavy rain was coming in from the west and the wind was blowing hard by the time she got back. Jan took a quick shower and changed from shorts to jeans and a cute tee shirt since she was working from home. She sat at her home office computer to begin another day of uncertainty; she needed to immerse herself in her work. She would never get the chance.

• • •

Damian and Caleb were waiting for the perfect opportunity to kidnap Jan but were still hoping for Marisa to show up so they could kill two birds with one stone. *Pun intended*, Damian thought. If Marisa did not show up soon they would have to consider other options. They would have to time any attempt to kidnap Jan perfectly. The dog had to be outside when they went in or they would have to shoot it.

• • •

Marisa walked the streets of Atlanta over night spending some time in a few local resturaunts whose bars were open until 2 a.m. She ate and drank a few glasses of wine slowly while reading a magazine trying to kill time. She was not sure on how or when to approach Jan. She knew Jan would try to turn her in. After sleeping on a park bench for a few hours she got up and went to a gas station rest room to wash up and brush her teeth and hair. She wanted to look halfway decent when she saw Jan. Without a cell phone Marisa's options to call Jan were limited. Marisa finally found an old pay phone at another gas station hanging on the wall just outside the store. She had two numbers for her, one the office and one the home office. She knew Jan did not give out her cell phone to clients.

Jan was deeply involved in an appellate brief when the phone rang. "Hello, this is Jan Bergin."

"Hello Jan, I am sure you were expecting my call. I'm in Atlanta. I have a lot to tell you and I need your help."

"Marisa! Are you alright? I have been worried about you." Jan was trying to remain professional but she was excited to finally hear from her.

"I'm not sure about anything right now. I need to see you. I think I am close to your house. If you give me your address I can get a cab and come over."

"Marisa, this is not a good idea. What will you do once you get here? I cannot be accused of harboring a fugitive."

"Jan, I need your help. Damian killed William and tried to kill me. I have nowhere else to turn."

"Alright, we will think of something together but I have to tell you that you will have to turn yourself in. I will help you do that but I cannot help you stay on the run. I already helped beyond what I should have." Jan was referring to the money she sent Marisa through the investigator. She justified sending the money by telling herself she planned to convince Marisa to turn herself in once she got to Atlanta.

"Okay." replied Marisa. She knew she would have to lie to Jan to get her to help and to have time to get to Damian. Marisa hung up the phone after talking to Jan and dialed a number she found on a sticker stuck to the pay phone for a local cab company.

Jan gave her the exact address and hung up the phone. She headed downstairs to put on a new pot of coffee. As she got to the bottom of the stairs, the front door was rammed open. Before Jan realized what was happening, she was in the arms of a six foot six linebacker. He had to weigh at least two hundred and fifty pounds. Jan was five nine but only weighed a hundred sixty five pounds; she was no match for this gorilla. Jan tried to scream for Ranger, but a piece of duct tape was slapped on her mouth by a second intruder. He pointed a .9mm with silencer at her head. The second man was about six feet tall with dark hair. She just knew it had to be Damian. She recognized him from Marisa's description. Jan frantically thought, "Where is Ranger?" She turned her head towards the kitchen and saw that the back door had blown shut. Ranger was clawing at the door but could not get in. Jan could see the desperation on his face. He was frantic. His bark was loud and stressed. He could not get to her. He would be devastated over not being able to help.

"Stop struggling, Ms. Bergin and quiet the dog. We are not going to hurt you. Is anyone else at home? Be honest, or this all will go badly," Damian said with no emotion in his voice.

Jan was being held in a bear hug by the big guy and could not move her arms. The more she struggled with her legs, the more he squeezed. She was having trouble breathing and felt her chest being pushed into her organs, heart pounding. She reluctantly shook her head yes to say she would comply.

Damian was not sure of her honesty so, for safety, he handcuffed Jan behind her back with a zip tie and put some rope anklets on her legs so she could only shuffle her feet one foot at a time. He took the tape off her mouth.

"There, Ms. Bergin, or can I call you Jan?" Damian said with distain in his voice. "Hell, I think I will call you Jan anyway. I don't need your permission."

"What do you want, Damian? Marisa is not here." Jan was frantic to try and resolve this before Marisa arrived. Jan had no way of knowing when that could happen.

"I know that. We have been watching you for a while now. She will be here, I know her well. We can wait. Shut your dog up or I'll shoot him." Caleb loosened the tape covering Jan's mouth.

Jan had no idea what to do. Marisa was walking into a trap. "Ranger quiet!" Jan said loudly but knew he would not be quiet. She knew he would not respond despite his training. His master was in danger and he could not save her.

·   ·   ·

Marisa flagged down a cab. With her hat and sunglasses she looked like a tourist. She got in the vehicle and gave the driver the address for Jan's residence. The house was only a few miles from where Marisa walked earlier. She felt bad that the cab fare was only six dollars so she gave the driver a twenty dollar bill when he let her off.

Marisa looked at the house. It was beautiful. She could see the front door was open. "That is strange," she thought. Jan knew she was coming, so maybe she left it open for her. Marisa approached the house with some trepidation. She walked up the front steps and tapped on the open door, she hesitated to just walk in.

"Hello, Jan, are you in here?" She could hear Jan's dog barking frantically.

Jan was being held by Caleb in the kitchen behind a door, the tape back on her mouth to keep her quiet. Damian could not risk Jan warning Marisa. Jan began struggling to get free but her hands were bound and Caleb had her in a bear hug again. Even if she could get loose, she could not run. Caleb's grip got stronger making it hard for Jan to breath. She knew Damian was hiding behind a closed door to the half bathroom on the ground floor just as you entered the house. Jan was desperate to try and warn Marisa to run but could do nothing but watch the inevitable.

As Marisa entered the house, Damian opened the door, which pushed Marisa aside. He grabbed her from behind, turned her around, and gave her a punch that knocked her out cold.

Jan let out a muffled scream in agony over what was happening, but to no avail.

"Jan, you can come with us quietly or I can do the same to you. What will it be?" Damian asked. "I will get what I want with or without your cooperation."

Jan nodded. The more she struggled, the more she feared for her life. Caleb let Jan go, took the tape back off her mouth and started to tie Marisa up.

"I would like to change my clothes and go to the bathroom," Jan said. If she had to go somewhere she needed to be dressed in clothes that could protect her if she was able to escape.

"If I let you get dressed, will you promise me you will not try anything. If you do, I will kill you, Marisa and your dog right here and now." Damian laughed and contemplated for a moment the possibility of killing them all right there and then, a burglary gone wrong, but he needed to know what Marisa had told the feds. He needed time, and they were too exposed in this neighborhood.

Jan knew he would not hesitate to kill them. "I understand," she said.

Damian helped Jan to the bedroom.

"Are you going to watch me, Damian?" Jan asked.

"I'm afraid so. I will take off your leg ropes first and then cut the zip tie so you can put your hands in front of you. When you get your pants on, I will reattach the leg ropes and you can put on a blouse. Then I will put a new zip tie on your hands."

Jan hated dressing in front of Damian but had no choice. He was pointing a gun at her head the whole time, smiling at what he saw, a strong, fit women in running bra and panties—his imagination running through what he would like to do, but had little time for.

Jan knew he enjoyed the control over her, she could see he was enjoying the moment. With no choice, she got dressed in a pair of comfortablepants designed for comfort and flexibility , a form fitting long sleeveshirt and some running shoes while Damian watched. All she knew was she and Marisa were in danger, and she needed to be as ready as possible to make a run for it.

"I would like to use the bathroom," Jan said.

"We do not have time for that," replied Damian.

"Well Damian, if I can call you that, which I think I will without your permission" Jan said sarcastically "it is either that or a messy smelly car." Jan was proud of herself for being snarky with him. At least she felt she was not totally controlled by his remarks.

"Nice Jan, I like feisty."

Damian checked out the bathroom before letting Jan in. No exit windows just a small stained glass slit for a little light.

"Go ahead, but be quick."

Jan went into the bathroom and quickly assessed the situation. She needed to let Kellie or someone know what had happened. She wrote in lipstick on the shower wall, "Kidnapped, Damian."

"Let's go, Jan, now!" Damian said with cold certainty. She knew he would kill her if she gave him the slightest reason. She quickly peed and flushed the toilet and closed the shower curtain just enough to avoid Damian seeing her message. She prayed someone would find it, and soon.

Caleb opened Jan's garage and brought their car into the space that Kellie vacated when she drove herself to the airport for her trip to Colombia. Damian helped Jan to the car and Caleb carried Marisa, she was still out cold. They laid both women in the back of the Jeep Cherokee. The back seats were down so they could lay full length on the floor. Caleb covered them with a blanket. The dark windows would keep anyone from seeing them. Jan could only pray they would not be killed.

•   •   •

William woke up around ten on Wednesday morning from the pain in his legs and back. He popped two of the pain pills he got from Rosey. He did not want to sleep this late but he was still not a hundred percent. He got dressed, had some coffee and breakfast, and checked out of the hotel. He decided to just show up at Jan's law office.

When William arrived, he was greeted by David. "Can I help you, sir?"

"Yes," William said. "I need to see Jan Bergin."

"I'm sorry, she's not in; she is working from home today. She doesn't see people without an appointment. I'd be happy to make one for you." David offered.

William began to get agitated. The pills, the pain, the events of the last few days were all he could take. "Look, I am William Herrera-Cardosas, Marisa's brother. I want to see Jan Bergin, and I want to see her now!"

David's mouth dropped open. "I thought you were dead!"

"Obviously not!" William said with anger. He was not angry at David, but Damian for trying to kill him. He finally let out his anger over the pain of betrayal.

"Okay, okay. I'm sorry but Marisa said Damian killed you. Do you have some I.D.?"

The only I.D. William had was the fake one with the name John Ramos. "No, I don't. You will just have to believe me."

William started to spit out the story of their daring escape. His anger showed as he told the story of Damian's help and then his attempt to kill him and his sister. David could see William was in physical and emotional pain. William finally broke down and cried. David just sat in silence, not knowing what to do or say.

"Look," David finally said to break up the situation, "I can try and reach Jan, she should be at home. She told me this morning that she would be working at home and said she was waiting to hear from Marisa."

David picked up the phone and dialed Jan's number. He let it ring at least ten times. If Jan was out she would have left the answering machine on. No one picked up.

"William, I can't reach Jan. It's not like her to not call in to tell me she is on her way out during the work day."

"Look David," William said with a slight edge to his voice, "I do not know Jan, but I know my sister: she is on her way to see Jan or already there. Damian is a desperate man. I suspect he too knows where Jan lives and is on his way there as well."

David became alarmed. "Should we call the police?"

"No!" shouted William. "That could get all of us arrested. Can you take me to Jan's house or give me directions?"

David was unsure of what to do. He was suspicious of William but afraid for Jan. All he could do was trust this guy and hope he did not get all of them killed. "OK, let's go. I will take you to Jan's house, it's not far."

David and William drove to Jan's residence. William cautioned David to drive around the block first to see if anything looked suspicious. David pointed out Jan's house. Nothing seemed amiss, so they pulled into the driveway and went up to the front door. David knocked but no one answered. He knocked again, harder this time. He could hear Ranger barking in the backyard.

"You better stay here, William; I have a key and will go in and check around. Besides Ranger knows me and may not let you in." When David put his key in the door he realized it was not locked, cautiously David opened the front door.

"Jan are you here?" David cried out. "Jan!".

William stayed at the front door while David went in. David could see there had been a struggle: the foyer table and lamp were on the floor. He could see through the kitchen to the backyard where Ranger was barking and clawing at the door. The poor dog looked worn out and distressed. David went through the kitchen to let Ranger in. He could see the outside of the door was torn to pieces where Ranger had worked so desperately trying to get inside the house. Ranger immediately bolted to the front door which David had closed. He started desperately barking all over again.

"Ranger come." David commanded. "Come!" Reluctantly Ranger came to David but would not stop barking or facing the front door. "What's going on boy? Where is your mom?" He pet Ranger's head trying to calm him down and then went upstairs to Jan's home office. Ranger followed David but kept looking back towards front door and stairs.

William could hear Ranger barking and decided to stay on the porch with the front door closed until David said it was safe to go in.

As David began looking at Jan's desk, he shuffled the papers and files around, nothing out of the ordinary except a card with the words "The Charity" written on it. He put the card in his pocket and walked down the hall to the bedrooms. As he got to Jan and Kellie's bedroom Ranger became more agitated sniffing the room as if something was not right. David looked around at the clothes on the floor but did not think there was anything unusual about that. Suddenly Ranger started barking again looking towards the master bath.

"Easy boy, what is it?"

David started looking around but could not see anything out of place. He looked at the shower curtain which was slightly open. . He was afraid to open the curtain trembling as he thought about what he could find there. As he slowly pulled back the shower curtain his mind flashed to the shower scene in *Psycho*. He was afraid he would find Jan's dead body or a blood soaked bathtub. He slowly pulled the curtain back. Instead of a body, he saw the scrawled, hurried message Jan had left. "Oh God!" he said out loud. He ran downstairs to the front door. Just as he was starting to open the door he realized Ranger was with him and William was outside. He could not let them meet as Ranger might bite William after experiencing whatever happened at the house. Ranger was agitated and would not likely welcome another stranger.

"Ranger, I hate to do this but I have to put you back outside. Come," he commanded. Ranger reluctantly followed David. He shut the back door and returned to the front door. "Come in, we have a problem, it looks like Damian kidnapped Jan and probably Marisa too if she was here."

William was dismayed; he knew what Damian would do. He also suspected that Damian would not risk killing them in the United States, he would take them out of the country now that his first attempt to kill Marisa had failed. But William had one advantage, Damian did not know William was still alive.

William knew Damian was desperate to know what Marisa had told the government before he killed her, and he needed to know what Jan knew about Marisa's case. There was a wealth of important details about the case in the government's files that Jan knew would help Damian avoid arrest and protect his precious drug business as well as the Vasquez family. William knew that if Damian could get this information and give it to the Vasquez family he would be a hero. This information would help him protect the family and his own fortunes while making him look good, even at the cost of killing three people. William had to find them before Damian killed Marisa and Jan.

"David, I need to get a flight to Colombia, South America. I need to get to Medellin and from there I can get a flight to the town where I think he will take them, a place he often goes to meet the Vasquez family."

"How do you know where to go, William? Shouldn't we call the police or FBI or something?" David said frantically.

"No, that could get them killed sooner. Marisa told me where Damian's hideouts are located and this is where the Vazquez family operates from. It is remote and very rural so no one bothers the family there and the community welcomes the work and income that is generated from the Vasquez family businesses

"You mean the drug business," David added.

"Yes and they have other businesses in the area, legitimate now, though started with drug money."

"Jan's partner, Kellie is in Medellin on a work assignment, she is a former FBI agent; could she help us? This seems so dangerous and way too real for amateurs," David said.

"The rural town they do business out of is called Turbo. It is one of the locations where the family homes and plantations are located for the growth of coca and marijuana plants. . Do you know where Kellie is and how to reach her?"

"Yes, let's go back to the office to make your flight arrangements and I can give you Kellie's information there. I can e mail her."

"What about the dog?" William asked.

"Don't worry, I'll come back to get him. I will take him to my house, he knows me. I babysit him when Jan and Kellie are on vacation or out of town for business."

• • •

Having already visited the city leaders in Apartado, Kellie was in Turbo, another rural coastal town nearby. . She was there with her two bodyguards and translator. She had spoken to the local bankers and community leaders in both cities regarding building factories in their area. They were all receptive to the ideas and were showing her land possibilities for such American ventures. The community leaders were excited about the prospect of starting to build a legitimate economy for such a remote area. Turbo seemed to be more suited for a factory due to its location near waterways.

In these remote areas of the country the streets were still dirt paved with hourse- drawncarts with tires for wheels as common as the fancy Mercedes and Lexus cars being driven or parked on the side of the road. Everyone seemed to be carrying a sidearm. There were some pearl handled six-shooters in Old Western style holsters but she could see that most men in town carried modern Glocks or nine millimeters. The women seemed to be oblivious to all of it, going about their daily business, whatever that was.

The hotel she stayed in was a one story, six room rundown building with chickens and pigs in the courtyard. As old as the hotel was, they were up to date on computer technology and e-mail though the only terminal was in the small hotel office. No executive suites or amenities, no bar or restaurant. The rooms were old and musty with a cement floor and one full size bed with a lumpy mattress. It wasn't the Marriott but the staff tried to make her feel special asking her every time they saw her if there was anything they could do to make her stay more enjoyable. She had taken four of the six rooms and the money she was spending for the overnight stay was probably more than the owner sees in any single month. They brought ice to her room and a bottle of Chivas Regal, though she never drank scotch.

Kellie and her group had been up since five in the morning flying in from Medellin for all day meetings. The citizenry of Apartado and Turbo wanted American commerce and products, but many admitted drug money had helped the region get their first school and hospital. It was a delicate matter to bring in foreign business. Some of the old timers who made their fortunes in the drug trade were uncertain about the local population with divided loyalties and shifting political power. Most of the police were corrupted but the new government was bringing in the army to help control the drug problem in the area. There was promise here in helping the locals with jobs in industry instead of working for the drug cartels. The difficulty is convincing the locals that wages in a factory are still better than the fast riches of the drug trade. Kellie got back to the hotel after a long day of meetings and viewing properties.

"Carla, I am going back to my room before our dinner meeting with the Mayor. You should get some rest. Tell the bodyguards to do the same," Kellie said to her translator, who had to be just as worn out as she was.

"I think that's a good idea," Carla replied. She translated the instructions to the bodyguards, Jorge and Garcia. They acknowledged with a "Si" and left to rest in their rooms.

Kelly took off her clothes and headed for the shower. In the shower there was a single pipe with no shower head. Below were hot and cold water knobs and a three foot high round bucket already filled with cold water. She turned on the hot and cold water only to get a trickle of cold water from the single pipe sticking out from the broken tile wall. After calling the front desk, she learned the water is shut off at six p.m., it was already eight in the evening of a long day. Primitive is all relative to what people think is more important than something else, Kellie thought. With a chuckle, she climbed into the bucket of cold water and took a cold sponge bath. Kellie was just happy to get the grime of the day washed off.

•   •   •

David and William were at the office making flight arrangements and looking at Jan's e-mail to see where Kellie was. David had a password to get Jan's home e-mail and found the message Kellie had sent from Medellin. David sent an urgent e-mail to Kellie. "Kellie, Jan and Marisa have been kidnapped by Damian. The brother thinks they are heading your way around Turbo. If you are in Medellin can you meet him somewhere? Advise where, that's all we know, Ranger is OK. I will keep him."

"William," David said, "the only flight I can get is tomorrow morning. I made the reservation, you are headed to Medellin, Colombia. Where will Damian take them?"

"I am not sure but . the Vasquez family owns a villa outside of Turbo that Marisa has spoken of before. She and Damian have gone there when things in the states were to hot. Damian may have trouble with the Vasquez family, but once he brings the girls there he will have no choice but to kill them or the family will. They may end up killing Damian as well for all the trouble he has created. The family was a little upset when he killed one of his off-loaders. I will contact you once I get to Medellin. I can make arrangements for a flight to Turbo from there. There are several during the day I can get on."

David sent William to a hotel near the airport by cab. while he paced the office waiting for a return e-mail from Kellie. He prayed out loud, "Kellie, get this quick wherever you are."

•   •   •

Damian and Caleb had been conversing in the front seat discussing how to get out of the city.

"Caleb, is the plane ready?"

"Yes, I texted Frank and he is filling the plane with fuel and will be ready when we get there. How are you going to get the girls on the plane without arousing suspicion from the office staff when we check in and file a flight plan?"

"They will never see them. We can drive the car up to the plane and tell the office staff we are loading some goods to fly to Texas. Why lie about that? We are going to Big Springs but will tell them we are headed for Lubbock. The flight plan is the same, we tell them we are going to Lubbock, Texas."

•   •   •

It was dark under the blanket but Jan could hear Marisa moan, she was coming to. Jan whispered, "You are all right Marisa, I am here with you."

Marisa recognized Jan's voice, "Where are we?"

"We are in Damian's car headed to an airport best as I can make out from listening to Damian and Caleb talking."

Jan lifted her head just enough to look out the darkened window. It appeared they were pulling into the private airport inside the city of Atlanta. Caleb dropped Damian off at the flight control office and pulled the Jeep up to a small jet plane to unload the girls. Caleb opened the back of the Jeep.

"OK girls here is how we do this, I am going to unbind your legs and rebind your hands in front of you. I will help you out of the car and into the plane, no screaming. Out here on the tarmac no one can hear you, and I would have to break your neck to keep you quiet, very messy," Caleb said sarcastically. "Quietly walk to the plane and get in, no sudden movement and keep your hands still."

"Caleb, your boss is crazy, if you are a part of this you will be held responsible for aiding and abetting in our kidnapping, assault and possibly murder. You could spend the rest of your life in jail." Jan pleaded.

"Nice try counselor, but I like life just like it is. Besides Alan is family. Blood is thicker than your lawyer jargon."

"Who is Alan?" Jan asked.

"Never mind, shut up and get out of the Jeep and into the plane!"

Caleb untied their hands from behind. He had a bunch of zip ties so all he had to do was cut the old ones and retie new ones in the front. Caleb put a gun in Jan's back to make sure she and Marisa knew he was serious.

Jan tried to help Marisa as she slowly pushed herself out of the back of the Jeep. Listening to Caleb call Damian Alan, Jan realized he may not be using his real name. How many names did this guy have, David Stone, Damian and now Alan? she thought.

As they were entering the plane, Jan looked around. No one was nearby. The main terminal and tower were several hundred yards away and no other planes seemed prepped for flight. She could only see one plane landing which meant the tower was busy attending to the landing of that plane and not concerned for what Damian and Caleb were doing. She knew no one would hear her or see that her hands were restrained. She tried to think of something to do but was afraid Marisa could not yet help herself and her efforts to get someone's attention could end up being useless, much less get them hurt or killed. Jan felt a deep ache in her stomach would she ever see Kellie again? She wanted to be able to say goodbye if she was going to die.

• • •

"Caleb," Damian said, "are we ready? I advised flight control of our destination to Lubbock, Texas, and asked for clearance. If our customs guy is working in Big Springs we should be okay. I did not tell them our final destination was another airport and then to Colombia."

Damian paid a lot of money for the plane, not to mention buying his way out of the country without having to be searched once he got to Texas. Using agents he could buy in various small airports was easy. Texas was in route to Colombia and a big state. He made this run frequently to avoid main-stream customs when he flew to Colombia to meet with the Vasquez family or Santos.

Damian's mind was moving a mile a minute with his plans to solve his problems with the feds and the Vasquez family. Damian knew he needed to be clear of United States soil before he decided what to do with Jan and Marisa. His main concern was to get everything out of them that they knew or told the government before he killed them. He needed a place to do that without interruption and a place where no one cared if they were dead. No one would ever find them where he was taking them. He knew Jan and Marisa would not give him details without some extra prodding. Damian's lips curved in a sinister slight smile of affirmation to his plans.

• • •

Frank was the regular pilot for Damian and the Vasquez family. He never questioned Damian's plan. He was paid well for his silence and skills and for being ready at any time. Frank taxied to the runway and took off. Caleb was acting as the co-pilot while Damian relaxed in the seats across from Jan and Marisa.

Mockingly Damian told Marisa and Jan to "buckle their seatbelts and put their seats and tray tables in the locked and upright position before takeoff."

Marisa finally spoke, "Damian, I loved you. Why are you doing this? Jan has nothing to do with you, let her go."

"Sweet naïve Marisa, you just don't get it. You have been compromised. I can't take a risk you will expose me or the family."

"Damian, please! The government doesn't know anything important. Please let us go!"

"Quiet now, you cannot persuade me. I like my life just the way it is and want to go on living it. You think you're my only girl?" Damian knew what he had to do to Marisa, and being cruel was just part of his game.

"I thought you loved me." Marisa began to cry.

"You are so stupid. I never loved you, I need a lot of women, but you were easy to manipulate and you liked the money so don't give me your sob story. Now shut up and enjoy the ride."

Damian did love Marisa but no one, not even her, was worth saving to protect his drug empire. Someday he would leave the Vasquez family and be his own boss. No woman would get in the way. Besides, finding out what the government knows will put him back in the good graces of Santos and the Vasquez family. He missed his opportunity to kill Marisa when he had it, so now he would make the best of his mistakes by getting more insight into the government's case against him.

•　　•　　•

Kellie finished her sponge bath. The water was filthy from a long day in the country but she felt refreshed. Turbo was dusty and humid. There was only a fan in the room so Kellie stood naked in front of it for a moment trying to cool down. She got dressed in lightweight black travel pants and white, short-sleeved linen blouse and white lightweight tennis shoes. Though she was already sweating from the humidity despite the shower she had more to do; so she headed to the front lobby.

"My laptop battery is recharging and I need to check my e-mail. Can I use the office computer for a moment?" Kellie asked the desk clerk who spoke some English.

"Yes, please." He pointed Kellie to a small office behind the counter. This was not a hotel like those in bigger cities or the United States. The hotel office room was old, with dirty carpet, dusty tables and dirty cloth chairs. It did, however, have a small air conditioner window unit that alone was worth the time to check e-mail. She could see the clerk had been on the net surfing for information on the American city of Denver, Colorado. Kellie figured he was in Colorado looking at real estate probably dreaming of a better cooler life.

Kellie booted up her e-mail and entered her password. It was easier to read this computer than her phone. She had twenty-seven e-mails, mostly from the company she was working for. One e-mail stood out; it was from Jan's law office but had in the subject box "emergency." Kellie hated messages like this; she thought the worst that maybe Ranger died or something terrible happened to Jan. All manner of thoughts started to swirl in her head. Her heart began to race as she opened the email. It was even more horrifying than she could imagine, the love of her life was in serious danger.

She read the e-mail several times while trying to figure out what to do.. She had to get a grip and start thinking like an agent again. Her heart pounding, she e-mailed David and said to have William meet her in Turbo, Colombia. Now she had to collect herself for the meeting tonight with the Mayor of Turbo. He was a very important man in this small town, likely a former, or present day drug dealer but, nonetheless, important for any business deals to move forward. She did not know what else to do since she needed to hear from William on what happened and how she could help. She would check her e-mail one more time before she went to bed, though sleep would be elusive tonight. It was horrible to be somewhere and not be able to do something or call on friends and colleagues to help. She was in the middle of nowhere in Colombia. These thoughts only made things worse. She had to wait for William to arrive to know how she could help find Jan. The thought of losing Jan consumed her.

• • •

Damian's plane landed in Big Springs, Texas, for refueling. The airport area used for small plances was not too busy. customs for personal planes was a small office not connected to the main terminal. Frank taxied to the area to clear customs which was required when leaving or entering the country.

Damian knew how to get things done. He got out of the plane and with one engine still running went to speak to customs. If his agent was on duty, he could bypass protocol. In many cities throughout the United States and elsewhere in the world you can pay off anyone for the right price. Caleb contacted the customs agent they knew and found out he was expected to be on duty when they arrived. The pilot remained in the cockpit per Damian's instructions. Caleb was to watch the girls.

Jan knew this could be the last chance they had to get out of the plane before leaving American territory. "Caleb, I need to go to the bathroom."

"There is a portable toilet seat in the back. Draw the curtain."

Jan knew he was right but tried again. "That is not easy to use and is not private. For Pete's sake let us go to a real ladies room and freshen up."

"No deal. Do it back there or pee in your seat," he replied.

Marisa heard all of this but felt defeated and could offer no resistance. "Jan," she said, "there is no hope. I know Damian will kill us. My jaw hurts and I'm tired."

Jan whispered to Marisa, "Stop talking like that. We have to stay alive. We need to think and stick together. Don't give up."

"Stop talking!" Caleb shouted.

•   •   •

Damian walked from the plane to the customs shed. There was a small office inside with a sliding window to see the planes coming and going.

"Good afternoon, is Charlie Sims in today?" Damian inquired of the customs officer at the window.

"Yes, but he is on break. Can I help you? I am Officer Brown."

"Well, I am taking my plane and family out of the country and I need to register the plane, give you a flight plan, and clear customs. I have been here before and dealt with Charlie."

"I can help you, where is the plane?"

Damian was not happy about this. In a small airport, it is not uncommon for one or two customs personnel to clear private planes after searching them. Damian could not risk a search by anyone. Damian needed his guy Sims; he paid him well for covering his trips in and out of Colombia. He would fly to any location Sims was assigned to.

"Can I just wait for Charlie?"

At this the agent got a little suspicious. "No, I will clear you; you got a problem with that?"

"No." Damian replied with frustration.

"Come into the office and let me see your passport, flight plan, and aircraft paperwork," demanded Brown. "Then I will inspect the plane."

Damian entered the office and handed Officer Brown his passport, flight log, Frank's pilot license and their flight plan. He looked at the picture and name and then he looked at Damian.

"You are David Stone?" he asked.

"Yes."

"I have heard of you through Charlie, you rich or something? Where are you headed?"

"We are headed to Medellin, Colombia and Frank Anders is our pilot," replied Damian. He also was not headed for Medellin but using that city would deflect the real destination and it was a big city, so less likely to draw suspicion.

"What is the purpose of your trip?"

"Business," Damian replied.

"What kind of business you in Mr. Stone?"

"I do not think that is any of your business. I keep my business private." Damian was getting frustrated with all the questions.

"Mr. Stone, we need to know why you are going to Colombia."

"I am working on an investment there with a local corporation." Damian lied. He was getting tired of this agent's questions.

At that moment Caleb came in the office while Brown was reviewing Damian's passport.

"Hey Alan, what's the delay? Oh, sorry, I mean David." Caleb caught himself too late and accidentally used Damian's real name.

"Caleb, shut up and get back to the plane!" Damian was furious. Leaving the girls alone with Frank was risky and now Caleb slipped and called Damian by his real first name. Caleb was the only person who knew his real name and that was only because they were half-brothers.

"Hey," said Officer Brown, "What's going on here? Who are you guys?"

At that, and without hesitation, Damian stepped around the counter where Brown was standing and before he could react pulled his nine millimeter handgun and hit Officer Brown in the face with the butt of his gun knocking him out cold. Brown crumbled to the ground.

"Sorry Damian. I wasn't thinking. The girls are locked in the plane trying to pee."

"Caleb this is inexcusable! What were you thinking coming in here? Hurry, tie this agent up and put him in a closet somewhere before anyone else comes by."

Caleb did as he was told as usual. Though Caleb hated being a bodyguard he loved the money and life Damian had given him. When he was with Damian he felt important even if he was only his half-brother. Caleb was the illegitimate son of one of Damian's father's many girlfriends. Only Caleb knew Damian's birth name was Alan Johnson, but ever since he left home he just used aliases. It was hard for Caleb to keep all his names straight in his head.

Caleb and Damian's father was a wife beater and a drunk. When Caleb was eleven years old, he watched Damian leave home at age sixteen and never look back. He knew Damian hated his life ever since his father got custody of him at the age of ten after his mother killed herself. When Damian left home, no one heard from him for over seven years. When he finally contacted the family his only interest was whether Caleb was still living in the house. Damian left his number and address for him and told him to call if he ever needed him. Damian took care of himself. Caleb wanted to be like his older half brother.

When Caleb was able to leave home at eighteen he contacted Damian to find out if he could get him a job. He found Damian in Florida driving a Lamborghini and wanted to know what he was doing that let him have such a nice car. He had no idea what his half-brother was into. Caleb had gone nowhere in his life and jumped at the chance to get away. His father didn't care about him or Damian and kept calling them losers. When he hooked up with Damian it changed his life, giving him money, women, and travel. As long as he was discrete and protected Damian, he could do anything he wanted. Caleb could have been a football player, instead he was a bodyguard and a damn good one, most of the time.

Caleb always did Damian's bidding so he cleared his head, tied up the agent and put him into a customs clearing warehouse closet. He found some duct tape in the customs counter drawer and shut the door after taping the agent's mouth shut. It would take time for someone to find him.

"Caleb, get back to the plane, I have a few more things I need to do here."

Caleb did as he was told as he already could tell Damian was not happy he had left the pilot on his own with Marisa and Jan.

Damian used the agent's own gun and his limp hand to make the shooting look like a suicide. He removed the tape on his mouth and the zip ties on his feet and hands. He wrote a quick note and left it on the counter. "I am sorry" is all that it said, no signature. Whoever found Officer Brown would think he committed suicide, at least for a while. Damian left the closet door unlocked.

• • •

Though Frank was supposed to be watching the girls, he was more interested in his flight preparations and was not really paying attention to them. Jan had to do something.

"Marisa, listen to me; we have to try and run. The stairway to the tarmac is too close to the cockpit and the pilot would see us if we tried to get out using that exit. There is a small emergency exit window over the wing we can try and open."

Marisa wanted to help, she was beginning to feel better and start thinking clearly again. "Okay Jan. I can try. I'm becoming an expert at this escape stuff. Let's go."

"Good, that's more like it. Now help me open the emergency exit."

Marisa and Jan's hands were tied but Marisa was able to reach down and untie Jan's legs which were restrained with rope ties, and then Jan did the same to Marisa. Removing the zip ties on their hands proved more difficult as they did not have anything to cut them off with. They would just have to run with them tied for now, this was their only chance. Both of them turned around to grab the top and bottom handle of the emergency exit.

"Lift it up Marisa and I will pull it in."

Marisa suddenly cried out: "He's coming!"

Jan looked out the opposite window and saw Caleb coming towards the plane from the main terminal. He was about a hundred yards away and Damian was not far behind. "Hurry Jan!" Marissa cried.

"I'm trying. Lift up Marisa, lift!"

Suddenly the door came loose and fell in as they pulled, knocking them both off their feet. Jan saw the pilot turn around just as they pulled the exit door into the plane.

"Let's go Marisa! Come on!"

They both crawled out the small exit onto the wing. "Jump!" yelled Jan.

As they both jumped from the wing Jan fell forward and rolled skinning her arms. Marisa landed hard on her feet and collapsed in pain.

"Damn, I think I sprained my ankle; go Jan, run!"

"No, you are coming with me." As Jan said this she looked around and only saw runway, a building where Damian and Caleb had gone, the pilot crawling out the exit door screaming, and some underbrush two hundred yards away across the tarmac. There was no place to hide.

Jan tried to help Marisa up. "Come on Marisa, try!"

Together they began running and hobbling to the underbrush.

"Hey, stop!" Frank shouted through the emergency exit.

Frank ran down the stair exit and started running towards the customs terminal yelling.

"Damian, Caleb help, they are escaping!" Frank was out of shape and knew he could not keep up with Jan and Marisa who were younger and in good shape.

• • •

Damian left fraudulent customs forms behind which should keep the authorities off his trail long enough to get out of U.S. air space. He could hear the shouting. Caleb was outside, already running towards the plane.

Caleb saw the pilot coming towards him screaming. "Caleb, they are escaping!"

"Go after them, Frank, you idiot; stop them!"

Caleb looked under to the plane as he was running towards it and saw the girls running across the tarmac to some trees across the runway. He could see they were having difficulty running. Caleb was in good shape, but they did have a head start.

"Stop!" Caleb shouted. "You can't escape, there is nowhere to run! Frank, help me catch them!"

As he approached Frank running toward him, Caleb grabbed Frank's arm and turned him around. "Frank, you need to help me get them."

Even though Jan and Marisa could hear the yelling they kept running. "Jan," Marisa said, "we can't outrun them."

"I know," replied Jan "but I want to try. Damian won't kill us now, he needs to know what you told the government and what my files say."

Jan did not want to give in but Marisa was not doing well. She was still not herself after being cold cocked by Damian and now with her sprained ankle Jan's only hope was that maybe someone would see them. The problem was the airport was spread out with runway, and multiple hangers. It was unlikely they would be seen in time to get someone to help them. The flight control tower was too far away to see them clearly. .

It wasn't long before Caleb and Frank caught up to them. Caleb grabbed them by the back of their shirts and jerked them both to the ground. Before Jan fell she kicked her foot backwards into Caleb's shin with the heel of her tennis shoe with just enough force to cause Caleb a moment of agony.

Caleb was winded and caught off guard. He grabbed his shin and screamed in pissed off pain. "You bitch!" Caleb cried.

Caleb let Jan go to grab his leg when he heard the familiar cold voice of Damian from behind. "Move one inch and I will kill you both."

Damian had his gun in his left hand and had his right hand in a fist getting ready to slug Jan when Marisa cried out: "Stop Damian, please don't hurt anyone else! It was my idea. She was trying to help me!"

Marisa was pleading with Damian to back off. Jan knew it was not the time for heroic smart ass replies though she wanted to tell Damian he was merely a punk and one that will be dead once the authorities caught up to them. The problem with saying that would be injury or death and the uncertainty of whether they would ever be rescued or found alive.

"You are right my love, there will be plenty of time for revenge. Get them in the plane Caleb and hurry before someone get suspicious. Caleb, you need to be more vigilant or I will beat you down in front of everyone. Frank you are useless, you let the girls escape."

"Well Damian, you can fly the plane yourself if you think I am useless. It was not my job to watch the girls. I did it for Caleb while he went to see why we were so delayed."

"Listen both of you, we get caught because one of you slips up we are all going to jail; only I will have more money and information to offer than either of you. If you follow my plan we get out of her, lay low and get back to business when we clean up this mess with Marisa and her lawyer."

Damian was angry with Caleb and Frank for creating this new mess. Things were getting too complicated. With all the killing he had already done and still planned to do, he would have to stay out of the United States for a long time. He would deal with that later. Damian could see some main terminal assistants had come out of their offices and were looking towards the plane and what was going on. Some started to walk towards them until Damian waived and headed for the plane. He pushed Jan and Marisa up the stairs, closing the jet door. Caleb picked up the emergency door and locked it back in place.

"Let's go Frank, get us out of here now!"

Frank knew he was a good pilot and had flown for the Vasquez family for years, never with drugs just people or money. He had been a Navy pilot and was used to landing and taking off quickly and on short runways. When he got out of the service he could not find a job that gave him the same thrill and adrenalin rush the service did, so he hooked up with some old drug dealers and was eventually connected to the Vasquez family. He had been flying for them for the past five years. Frank had been assigned to Damian because of his drug and money success for the family. Frank had flown Damian all over the United States and foreign destinations particularly Colombia and France. Damian had taken Marisa to Turbo, Colombia, where the Vasquez family lived and introduced her to them showing off his connections and experience. He was fond of spending a great deal of time on the southern beaches of France or rather what is internationally known as the French Riviera. He did what he was told, but if the family knew what he was doing now, they would not approve. He would let them know in good time.

Frank taxied the plane to the runway. He waited for clearance as if everything was normal.

"Tower, we are ready for takeoff," Frank advised.

"What is going on down there? we noticed some commotion, please advise." came the controller's reply.

"Nothing to worry about, just a family argument, ready for takeoff." Frank repeated trying to get the controller to let them go.

The air traffic control tower had no idea what had occurred in the customs office. Agent Brown never had a chance to clear them or to advise the tower of their destination. This was arousing suspicion, but would take too long to investigate.

"We have cleared customs and filed our flight plan, ready to go." Frank said again.

Frank decided to just go. Before Frank received the okay he had taxied and was into his takeoff run. There really was no one to stop them anyway. Frank had the plane in the air in minutes. There were no law enforcement planes in the area and it was unlikely the controllers would call the military or that they could even get a plane to locate them once in the air. Frank shut off all communications and GPS tracking devices to keep them as undetectable as possible. Radar could see him for a while but once he left American airspace his plane would be lost.

• • •

William arrived in Medellin and called David from the airport. He was still stiff from his injuries and had trouble thinking from taking the pain pills.

"David, where do I go from here?"

"I got an e-mail from Kellie: she is in Turbo and wants to meet you there. Can you get there?"

"Yes, there are flights out of here regularly on Sam airlines. It is already five in the afternoon here and too late to get a flight. I need to get some rest so will catch a red eye flight tomorrow. E-mail Kellie what I look like and tell her to meet me at the Turbo airport tomorrow at nine in the morning." William knew time was not on their side but he had to get some rest, he was too weak to keep going.

David sent another e-mail to Kellie and received hers. "William is going to stay in Medellin tonight. Will meet you at the Turbo airport tomorrow at nine in the morning arrival Sam airline flight 238, good luck. I am here if you need me. I love you both, so please get Marisa and Jan, come home safe: love, David."

David could only wait and worry. He went home after picking up Ranger and wondered what he should tell the clients and judges. He decided first thing in the morning he would send out a notice of a family emergency and change court dates for at least a week; after all it was basically the truth. He could only pray this nightmare would end by then. Jan and Kellie were his family, he was there when they adopted Ranger and when they were married. He would not know what to do without them.

•   •   •

William arrived in Turbo on time after spending the night in Medellin. As he cleared the terminal he began looking for a woman who matched David's description of Kellie. Five foot nine, hazel green eyes, light brown hair, shoulder length, a slim athletic build. She was a bike rider and tennis player, so she would also be tan. William looked around; most of the people he saw were clearly of Colombian descent and did not seem to be looking for anyone.

Kelli stood back near the luggage retrieval area and watched the comings and goings of passengers. She could see most of the passengers knew where they were going. Only one person looked lost. "William," came a cautious voice from behind him. Startled he turned around to see a woman meeting the exact description of Kellie. "Kellie?" he inquired.

"Yes," she replied. "Let's go somewhere we can talk."

"How did you know who I was? I don't look like the picture David e-mailed from my identification."

"Call it the FBI training and good old fashion female intuition, it's a killer combination."

"Who are those guys?" William asked, pointing to three people standing nearby looking at them suspiciously.

"That is my translator and two bodyguards. If we get along I will send them back to the hotel." Kellie was not about to meet William, a major player in the drug world especially in Turbo, without some backup.

Kellie had already scoped out the small town of Turbo and knew of a small restaurant where they could talk. She rented a gold colored Jeep Grand Cherokee from the local banker. Her company was well known in the region, so the banker gladly gave his car to Kellie for as long as she needed it for a fee. He sought favor with her for the money she could bring to the region by approving any land lease in the area for factory construction and a little extra for his family.

Kellie was an unusual business person for the area. In this part of Colombia they had never seen a white American female doing business. Most of the town's politicians had once worked in the cocaine processing factories or were in a drug family. There were some banana plantations, but compared to the income from the drug business, it was hard to match the money someone could make processing the coca leaf paste into powder cocaine or pulling marijuana plants for drying and processing.

When they arrived at the open air restaurant, Kellie pointed to a table near the corner. It was private and looked out over the main dirt road leading through the town. She could see her bodyguards, and they could see her from their location at the car. Kellie had sent Carla back to the hotel for the day since William spoke good English. She ordered two beers in Spanish: "Dos cervesas, por favor."

"Tell me what you know about Damian and where he is going," requested Kellie.

William gave Kellie the details of the escape and what happened in the harbor. "When Damian found out he did not kill Marisa, it now appears he thought it would better to determine what she told the government about his operation before killing her. I know she was trying to protect me by holding out for a deal with the government that would release me from any threat of jail so she started cooperating. This has put her in grave danger with Damian. She is being unrealistic by trying to keep me out of jail, the government needs me to help break up Damian's organization and the Vasquez Family connection with him. They also need me to corroborate Marisa's story. I want to help Marisa to make up for my wasted life. She is in this position mostly because of me that is why we developed the escape plan. I had no idea Damian wanted to just kill both of us. I think Jan is going to be collateral damage."

Inside, Kellie's heart raced with fear over the possibility of losing her partner. She listened to every word William spoke. He told her about the escape, his near-death experience and Damian's deceptions.

"Damian thinks I'm dead. Jan is another way for him to get to Marisa. Damian knew that Marisa would go see Jan for legal advice after he tried to kill us. He knew Jan was our only source of support both legally and practically." William said.

"Where will Damian take them?" Kellie asked.

"Marisa told me about a villa the Vasquez family owned up the coast from here on the water. Damian often stayed there with Marisa when things were too hot in the U.S., or he did not want to travel to Europe, or was summoned by the family to discuss business. I expect him to take them there. He does not want the Vasquez family knowing about this mess until he cleans it up. He is ruthless, but they are worse and will not tolerate incompetence. Damian has made a lot of money for the Vasquez family and for now they still trust him. If the Vasquez family found out what he has done or might be about to do, they would probably kill him, and not quickly. They have several villas in the area but own a farm farther away where they spend most of their time. I believe Damian will take them to one of the villas. The only one I know is about fifteen miles outside of town."

"What will he do with Jan and Marisa when he gets to the villa?" Kellie asked getting increasingly concerned for their safety as she realized Damian was a cold-blooded killer.

"I think he will try to motivate them to talk and tell him everything they know about Marisa's case and what she told the government. Damian probably does not believe what Marisa has told him so far. He will also want Jan to tell him what she knows from the government discovery documents and the meetings Marisa and Jan had with the government. Then, he will likely kill them both. He will take this vital information to the Vasquez family which will buy him time with any discontent they may have over his actions. That information would reveal who some of the other informants are against the family so they can take action against them, preventing anyone from ever having the opportunity to testify against the family."

Kellie sat in silence afraid to even think of such a possibility. A waitress brought them their beers. Kellie knew Jan and Marisa were in serious danger. She had worked drug cases before and the bigger the drug organization, the more they were willing to kill or torture those who threatened its existence.

Kellie broke the silence, "How will we find this villa?"

"I don't know," replied William. "Marisa once described it but I have never been there. I have no idea where it is but maybe someone in Turbo can help."

Kellie thought for a moment and realized she had no choice but to contact locals to get information. Her biggest concern was how to get them to trust her. Asking questions about Damian and the Vasquez family could be risky.

"I need to meet with some of the locals, and you need to be with me William. We have to get them to trust us and help us find Damian's hideout. If we don't mention what we are doing or why we need this information, someone might help us."

"Ok," replied William. "Marisa has been here before. People will know her name, but you have to get rid of the bodyguards, and I can translate for you. Kellie, I want the same thing you want, I want my sister back and you want your partner. I am not the problem, Damian is."

"I know William. I am going to have to trust you."

With that, Kellie and William went to her bodyguards, and through William's translations told them to go back to the hotel, leave the Jeep and wait for further instructions. Kellie could see they were not happy and looked at William with suspicion. They asked if Kellie was sure and she reaffirmed she would be okay. She did not want them to follow her or know what she was doing. Kellie believed the banker was a good place to start asking questions.

"Ok, what now?" William asked.

"We go to the bank and see what my friend there knows. He was once a drug trafficker but now he has his own bank. The best kind of money laundering," Kellie said with a slight grin.

Kellie's FBI training was becoming more important than she expected. She was a good agent and was involved with intelligence gathering on cartels and smugglers. Just before leaving her post with the FBI, she was involved in gathering information on terrorists. She left the FBI for more money but also to get away from the stress and spend more time with Jan. Now she was threatened with losing the very things in her life that gave her joy and happiness. Kellie had to keep her head and work from her training, not from her heart.

Together Kellie and William left the restaurant and headed for the El Banco de Colombia to talk to Andrew Castagno. He knew everyone in the area and was the most likely banker for the drug dealers, including Damian and the Vasquez family. His connections went back to his days as a narcotics trafficker. When he stepped down from his daily drug activities, his son took over that part of his family business. Though Andrew was now legitimate the family was still involved with the drug trade. Andrew would know who to talk to.

•　　•　　•

The plane left Texas in the late afternoon. The flight to Colombia took most of the night. The sun was coming up through the window of the plane and Jan could tell they were no longer in American air-space. She had not slept much on the flight though she was dog tired. She could not stop thinking of ways to get out of this mess, but knew running was not a good option now with Marisa's sprained ankle. They had no ability to overpower any of the men, and they had no idea where they were or what was about to happen. Jan could only think of how upset Kellie would be to find out she was kidnapped and killed. No matter what, Jan was determined to try and get away if she had the chance.

Damian changed places with Caleb. He was now in the co-pilot seat and Caleb was relegated to watching the girls. Damian was busy reviewing landing coordinates with Frank.

Damian slapped Caleb around in front of the girls when they took off. His face was red, and he was angry, embarrassed, and hurt. He hated Damian for belittling him in front of others but he knew he had screwed up.

"Caleb, why are you doing this?" asked Marisa.

"Be quiet. I have nothing to say to you two."

"Yes, you do. Help us and we will help you." Marisa thought she could get Caleb to help them, especially after Damian embarrassed him. Right now he hated Damian.

Jan also hoped Caleb's embarrassment would make him easier to be influenced but not on the plane. They would have to find a time to try and make Caleb an ally instead of an enemy when they got on the ground. How, when and where were the unanswered questions.

"Caleb, where are we going?" asked Jan.

"To Colombia," he replied.

"Where in Colombia?" she pushed.

"Turbo," he replied.

Jan and Marisa looked at each other. Somehow they had to get word to someone where they were headed.

"Marisa, does anyone else know where we might be going?" asked Jan in a whisper.

"William might have because he knew Damian took me here before but he's gone."

Jan began to ponder whether David, her legal assistant might look in the files at her notes for help. In the meantime Jan had to figure out what they could do once they arrived at their destination. She did not want to die in some small town in a foreign country where no one would be looking for her or could likely find her. She did remember that Kellie was going to Medellin and some other small Colombian towns, but Kellie never told her which towns, just that her base would be in Medellin and she would be there most of the time.

• • •

Kellie took William to the bank to speak with Andrew. Andrew Castagno was an influential man in this small town. He could speak fluent English and was revered as a man of the world who had many American connections, some for drugs and some for legitimate business. When Kellie told him what was going on, he hustled them to a back room.

"Kellie, you know I would do anything to help you but the people you speak of are very dangerous; I cannot betray my own people. Such betrayal could mean my death or death to my family. I still have to live here. I like doing business with you, but I cannot risk my own success or the safety of my family. I am dependent on the local economy and other drug family money."

"I know Andrew, but lives are at stake here. You must tell me where this Damian Garrison stays when he is here meeting with his boss. Where is the Vasquez family compound?"

"Damian and the Vasquez family hold a great deal of influence in these parts. Everyone fears Damian and knows he works for the Vasquez family who will stop at nothing to protect their interests and security."

Kellie was desperate, Jan was her life; she could not fathom a life without her partner; she would find her, no one could stop her.

"Andrew, what will it take for you to help us?"

William decided to speak up. "Look Mr. Castagno, I worked for Damian. I know when he is here he stays at one of the Vasquez family villas up the coast. We only want you to tell us what villa Damian might go to, not where the Vasquez family compound is."

"Why do you need this information?" Andrew asked.

"The less you know the better. Suffice it to say we have loved ones who are in danger and need to find them." For a former drug dealer, Castagno was not very confident, Kellie thought.

"Damian will know I told you, he will kill me!" whined Castagno.

"Not if we kill him first." Kellie could not believe what she was saying. As an FBI agent she had fired her gun only once while undercover on a narcotics task force case. She never had to kill anyone. For the first time since this whole mess started, she realized she would kill anyone who tried to hurt her or Jan.

"Ok here's the deal," Kellie offered. "I will promise you the company we are working for will use your bank when they set up a factory in this region. We will use you for funding and banking," Kellie was taking a big risk in saying this as she had yet to get approval from the company she was working for that they were even going to start a factory in this area.

"How do I know this will happen?" replied Andrew.

"Because I will do whatever it takes to get you the business, it is my call." Kellie lied, but did not care , she he had to make Andrew believe her.

Andrew hesitated but decided to help as this would bring millions of dollars and legitimate work to the region, and he will be even more respected.

"The house you are most likely looking for belongs to the Vasquez family and is used for out of town guests. It is about fifteen miles north of Turbo on the coast. That is there closest villa so I would suggest trying there first. It is yellow in color and looks over the water. There are guards on the premises. Take the main road north of town and turn left on the dirt road at about the fourteen mile mark on your odometer. Now leave, if something goes wrong do not come back here." Andrew wanted to be a big American business connection, but he was more afraid of the drug families. He wanted them to leave quickly.

"Thank you for your help," replied Kellie.

"Just leave now" Andrew opined.

As William and Kellie were escorted to the front door of the bank, they heard the sound of gunfire and breaking glass. Instinctively Kellie fell to the ground pulling William with her. As she turned to see what had happened she looked into Castagno's terrified eyes. He was staring out the front window of the bank as if he were looking at a monster. Then Kellie saw the red stain growing on Castagno's white shirt. She looked into his eyes only to see them rollback in his head as he collapsed in death. Another shot rang out and another window shattered. Kellie crawled under the broken window for cover motioning for William to follow. Together they crouched behind a narrow wall between the door and window trying to figure out what happened. Other customers in the bank were on the floor screaming. Tellers were ducking behind the bulletproof glass that separated them from the main lobby of the bank.

"What was that?" cried William.

"Someone appears to know what we are doing and doesn't like it. We have to get out of here. We need to go back to Castagno's private office in the back of the bank. There is a back exit door in his office that leads to a side street. Follow me."

They began to creep along the floor to Castagno's body. As they passed him, Kellie saw the butt of a gun sticking out of the side of Castagno's belt just under his open jacket. She reached into his belt and took it. He would not be needing it anymore. It was a ten shot nine millimeter Glock, ten in the clip, one in the chamber. She stuck the gun in her back waste band and kept crawling towards Castagno's office. Another shot rang out, this time even closer, hitting the wall just above them.

"Hurry William!" Kellie yelled.

William was still in pain from his burns and the pain pills were wearing off, but despite the pain he was already inside the door to Castagno's office. Kellie was right behind him. As she entered the office she closed the door only to hear another bullet go through it.

"Go William, go!"

Together they got up and ran for the exit door. They didn't dare look back as Kellie could sense whoever was shooting was coming after them.

Out on a side street Kellie responded like the agent she was. There were a few parked cars but no traffic. She pulled out the Glock she had taken off of Castagno's dead body and took a defensive stand looking in both directions pointing the gun in front of them in case she had to shoot.

"The Jeep is out front, William. Let's creep up to the corner and see if we can get to it without getting ourselves killed. I will go first."

Kellie slowly approached the corner of the bank. With her back to the wall, gun drawn in front, she peered around the edge of the building. She could see the usual people on the street had taken cover and were running away from the bank. She could see the Jeep and knew they had to get to it to escape.

Kellie turned to William to tell him her plan. He was standing right behind her breathing heavily. As she turned the back exit door they had just come out of opened. Standing in the doorway was her bodyguard.

"Am I glad to see you, Pablo. What happened out there? We need to get out of here. Can you help?"

"Of course, Ms. Kellie, come with me," he said in perfect English.

Kellie didn't know he could speak English at all. During the whole time her body guards were with her she was using her interpreter to speak to them. The tone of Pablo's voice was stiff and his mannerisms seemed hesitant. He just did not look like a person who had just seen shots fired into a bank at the very person he was assigned to protect. As she looked at him her instincts told her something was not right. She saw that he was holding a weapon down by his side and realized he could either be the one doing the shooting or he pulled his weapon when he heard the gunfire. She was not sure which option was true. He started to raise his hand but William was in the way. Her gut told her that her bodyguard knew what was going on and may have warned someone about what she and William were looking for. Pablo or someone he knew must have killed Castagno.

Kellie's mind was racing. In a split second of thought, and her training, Kellie grabbed William's shirt with her left hand and pulled him backwards, she moved her right hand over his shoulder and in front of his backward falling body pointed her gun directly at Pablo and shot him in the head. He raised his gun just enough to get a shot off grazing skin on William's side.

William fell to the ground from Kellie's maneuver screaming in pain.

"I've been shot Kellie!"

"Get up William! We have no time, move!" Kellie could see a trickle of blood starting to show through William's shirt. She helped him up.

As William got up off the ground he groaned, "God, this is too much. He was trying to kill us!"

"Are you okay, William? Can you move?"

"It hurts like hell, but I think I am okay, he just grazed me. I can feel the blood but not a hole." William pulled up his shirt to see a bleeding cut on his left side but not a gunshot hole. He would bleed, but not die.

"Come on; we don't have time to wait for someone else to show up or the authorities to question us."

"I am right behind you, let's go!" William forced himself to move out of pure survival adrenaline.

They ran out into the street to the Jeep. There was a lot of chaos still going on. To the average observer they both looked like everyone else, running for cover or trying to get away from a dangerous situation. There were people running out of the bank while the local police were running toward the bank to see what had happened. Kellie knew no one saw her shoot Pablo, but she could not know if anyone would put together her visit with the bank and the gunfire. She could only hope the chaos of the situation kept her and William from being remembered. They made it to the Jeep and peeled off. She had no idea where her other bodyguard was or if he too was a danger to them. In the car Kellie saw a couple of old rags on the floor of the back seat.

"Grab those rags behind you and put pressure on your wound," Kellie said.

William took one of the rags which was actually a small old cotton blanket with holes in it. It looked like it was used for a hand rag and was pretty dirty but he had no choice. He tore a long narrow piece and tied it around his midsection to stop the bleeding. He took the prescription bottle of pain medication from his pocket and popped two more pills. The blood stain on his shirt was not too noticeable as he was wearing a black shirt with blue jeans. It just looked wet.

•　　•　　•

David was on hold with Jake Harden the Assistant United States Attorney assigned to Marisa's case in New York. David had not heard from anyone since

William arrived in Turbo to meet Kellie. He knew Jan and Marisa were in danger and that William and Kellie were headed in the same direction. He did not know if he was doing the right thing by calling Harden, but he felt this thing that was going on was bigger than him and he was afraid for the safety of his friends. He needed to get some help.

"Mr. Harden, this is David Bowers calling from attorney Jan Bergin's office. I am not sure how to begin but I think I need your help."

David proceeded to tell Jake what happened after the escape. He told him about the kidnapping and Damian trying to kill Marisa and William. He did not want to tell him about Kellie and William hooking up in Colombia as he was afraid to let Jake know where they were. David thought Jake Harden might be more interested in arresting William and Marisa than finding Jan. David told Jake he thought Damian was intending to kill Jan and Marisa after getting all of the information from them about what the government knows about him and the Vasquez family.

"I am not sure what I can do" Jake offered. "Marisa told us some of what she was doing but never got into the rest of the story before she escaped. She did not want to give up her brother. She told us about a guy named David Stone, not Damian Garrison."

David was not sure how much he should tell Jake. He was a reasonable prosecutor, but he also was ambitious so he was not going to give anyone a break if it interfered with his success now or in the future.

"Look Mr. Harden, I can tell you that Damian and David Stone are one and the same person. Have you heard of the Vasquez drug family?"

"Yes, they are a high priority on our list of drug family cartel targets. Getting them would be significant to helping the war on drugs."

"Well," replied David, "Garrison is the direct link with the Vasquez family drug business. Marisa and William know the connections here in the United States and Colombia."

"That is interesting. Marisa never disclosed that connection, just some information on this David Stone. Do you think Marisa will turn herself and her brother in? She needs to tell us everything if we help her since we tried to help her in the first place but she let us down by orchestrating her escape."

Jake was no fool. Getting this David Stone, or Garrison person, and the Vasquez connection, would be politically advantageous to his career. If he could pull off taking down one of the drug families he would be in line to be appointed as the United States Attorney and not just an assistant. From there he could do anything, including run for governor or senator of New York.

"Marisa has not made it easy to help her, the escape looks bad for all of us. Okay David, here is what I will do," replied Jake. "I will call the DEA task force working with the local government in Medellin, Colombia. I will ask them if some agents could go to Turbo and see what they can find out. I can't promise anything without more information, but I will try."

"Thank you Mr. Harden, I hope I have done the right thing. Jan would fire me if she thought I breached any attorney client privileges."

"I think this situation is serious and Jan and Marisa are in grave danger. I am sure she would want the help. I like Jan, she is a good attorney despite our differences. Goodbye David, I will be in touch."

David hung up the phone. Ranger was sitting beside him. "Well boy, all we can do is wait. I know you are worried too." Ranger nuzzled David who obligingly scratched behind his ear.

•　　•　　•

Jake Harden wanted to find Marisa. After all, her daring escape had made him look foolish. He picked up the phone to call special DEA task force agent Roberto Barto . He knew about Marisa's case as the intelligence on the Vasquez family was information he was working on in Colombia He was stationed in Medellin, and heavily involved with cases that affected the United States that came out of Colombia. He had the connections to help and spoke fluent Spanish.

"Roberto this is Jake Harden. I just got the best call of our careers." Jake proceeded to tell Roberto all that he knew.

"What do you think we can do? I am willing to help Jan, but not at the expense of not arresting Marisa, the brother, and possibly this David Stone or Damian Garrison guy and maybe even the patriarch of the Vasquez drug empire; that would be a windfall for us and put me back on top."

"How do you know that Jan is not involved with this mess, Jake? We could use Jan as a potential suspect and really get some support for finding them. Think how much publicity we could get arresting a prominent defense attorney gone bad."

Roberto would love to arrest a criminal defense attorney. They were all the same, always trying to manipulate the case by putting words in agents' mouths when they testified in court and challenging procedures to get guilty clients off. Sometimes agents had to say things that were not a hundred percent true to support a conviction. He hated attorneys who made him look foolish on the witness stand. Even if he was not always truthful, most defendants were guilty of something.

"I gave her assistant my word I would help." Jake replied. "Jan is a good lawyer, we may disagree on case issues but she does her job protecting client's constitutional rights. I have no evidence Jan was involved in the escape."

Roberto did not discuss his feelings on this matter any further. He knew what he wanted to do, and now he was being given a reason to do it. He let Jake believe he was all for helping find Jan and Marisa.

"Ok Jake, I will get with my partner and fly over to Turbo to see what we can do."

After hanging up, Roberto set a plan in motion that would result in the killing of a major drug dealer. If his companions happened to die in the gunfight such is the risk. Collateral damage is always a risk for the DEA and the drug lords. Everyone knows the players and the game. Roberto was excited, he could get rid of some serious scum without having to deal with the Constitution or the slow moving American justice system. He would probably get a promotion in the process.

• • •

Kellie and William were leaving the city of Turbo. They were traveling on a lonely dirt road heading away from the town. All that was visible on each side of the road were banana plantations. No one would know where they were if something happened to them. Kellie regretted not e-mailing David about their plans as they developed. Then again, everything they were doing was spontaneous. Kellie had no clue about what she would do next or what they could expect.

As they were driving along the road they hoped would lead to Damian's hideout, a dark green four door military style Humvee with four people inside suddenly pulled in front of them causing Kellie to have to break hard and skid across the dirt road. Kellie was just able to stop before going over the edge of the road into a ditch.

"What is this, the Wild West?" Kellie shouted. "We first get shot at and now this. Are you all right William?"

"Yes. What do you think this is about?" William asked. .

"I have no idea. I know some Spanish but you better do most of the talking," Kellie said. "These guys look like military and may be more receptive to a man and someone who speaks the language fluently. Just listen to them and let me know what they are saying. We can't afford to lose any more time."

As Kellie and William were talking, three young men, none of them appearing to be over the age of twenty-one, got out of their truck and approached Kellie and William. They were all carrying AK47 assault rifles and dressed in military olive green uniforms.

One of the young men walked up to Kellie's window on the driver's side. He acted very nervous and began talking rapidly in Spanish. Kellie could figure out he was demanding papers and to know why they were in this area. William replied in Spanish that they had been in town but there was some trouble there. He told them he was looking for a friend's house and was going to surprise him with a visit.

A second military-dressed, gun-toting person came up to the passenger side where William was sitting. He demanded to know where they were from. This person had the military markings of some kind of officer, though he too did not look any older than the others. William repeated what he had already said and added that they were from America. When he was asked about Kellie he told them she was his cousin. This did not seem to be enough. The military police were acting very unsure of themselves. Kellie was concerned that at any moment they could get trigger happy and kill them. No one would know what happened to them. They could end up being human fertilizer for the banana plantations they were looking at, no one was around, no cars, no houses, not a semblance of life anywhere.

•   •   •

"Damian, we are getting close to the border, what do you want me to do?"

Damian listened to the pilot's question in the headsets they were wearing. The cockpit was too noisy to hear a conversation without them. They could also hear the air traffic controllers when they flew over Colombian airspace. They had been able to cover their tracks during the flight over different airspace by identifying their destination. Usually, if a plane was continuing on, the controllers were not too interested. By the time most were getting overly curious they would be out of range or the controllers would stop trying to contact them turning their attention to other flights. There was some concern that a military plane may try to intercede if they did not answer once they got into Colombian air space.

"Tell the air traffic controllers we are coming in from the states and will clear customs and ground at the Turbo airport," Damian instructed Frank. He had no intentions of landing at the Turbo airport.

Damian was concerned about running into Santos and the Vasquez family. He knew they would be angry over what was happening but he needed to know how much Marisa and Jan knew before killing them. He decided not to contact anyone when he arrived until he could resolve the problem. If he could bring good intel to the family, all his actions would be forgiven.

"Frank, land on the usual grass runway about ten miles out of Turbo. Here are the coordinates." Damian pointed to the topographic map he had been looking at and handed the pilot written specific flight coordinates for the private field the Vasquez family had built in the jungle to avoid detection.

"Damian are you sure you want to do this?" asked Frank.

Frank was now having second thoughts about ever getting involved with Damian. Somewhere in the back of his mind he knew he would never be able to leave the business without losing his life or going to prison.

"Just land this plane. You have been working for us for a long time; you have no other options."

To Frank, Damian's voice inflection was clearly meant as a threat."Look Damian, I can land but what you are doing is going to get us all killed. I want to make sure I get out of here."

"Frank, you need to know that you will land and land safely or you will not get out of this plane alive."

"Easy Damian, you need me as much or more than I need you. I am the only one who can fly this bird. You kill me, we crash, plain and simple."

Damian grabbed the pilot's arm and jerked it so hard the pilot was forced to turn, wincing in pain.

"Listen you piece of garbage I will kill you and crash this airplane. Killing everyone on board will solve my problems. Don't give me a reason to do something tragic. Do not test my resolve."

Frank decided not to discuss the situation any further. He realized Damian was crazy enough to kill them all. Even if he wasn't serious, he did not want to provoke the situation further while he was flying. He pulled his arm away. He would wait until there was a better opportunity to get out of there and leave all of them behind.

Frank found the coordinates Damian gave him. He could see the cut grass in the middle of an area of thick underbrush. The runway was short, it would be a fast hard landing. He put the plane in a nose down run, slowed his speed and pulled up just as he got to the ground, landing hard just like in the Navy on the aircraft carriers. He immediately throttled back and pressed hard on the brake, flaps up. The runway was short, but Frank had just enough room to stop. It was at least longer than an aircraft carrier. He turned the plane around for a fast takeoff if needed.

• • •

William and Kellie were instructed to get out of their vehicle. As they did one of the military police clicked off the safety to his AK47 and pointed it at them.

"Por favor!" cried William, raising his hands as if to give up. The last thing they needed was a hot-headed kid with a machine gun.

William started speaking rapidly in Spanish trying to keep their attention away from over-reacting. All of them were acting very nervous. Kellie did not want anyone to get trigger happy.

Kellie also raised her hands. She was afraid they would search her and find the gun stuck in her back waistband under her shirt.

"William, what's going on?"

"Un momento," he said to the police. "They are telling me they want to see our passports. They are military police but heard over the radio of trouble in Turbo."

Kellie and William slowly pulled their passports from their back pockets. All guns were pointed at them. Kellie kept her passport and wallet on her when out of the country no matter where she was or what she was doing. This way if anyone broke into her hotel room, she would still have her passport and money to get home.

William handed his passport over first. The lead officer slowly looked over the contents of William's passport and then the front picture of him. Although William's passport was American, he could see the issuing location was not the United States but Puerto Rico. William had no idea how to explain to these out of touch police, who had little training or knowledge of other countries, that Puerto Rico was a commonwealth of the United States and its citizens enjoyed the same status as all Americans.

As the officer looked over William's passport, another officer grabbed Kellie's passport and opened it to the front. Kellie had her passport issued in Washington D.C.

"Un diplomatica?" came a question from the officer holding Kellie's passport. He repeated it. "Una diplomatica?"

Kellie realized that the officer thought that Kellie had to be a U.S. Diplomat if the passport was from Washington D.C. People in other countries know that Washington D. C. is the seat of power for the U.S. government and where the President of the United States lives. It was just by happenstance Kellie got hers from there.

"Si" replied Kellie on impulse. "Si, un diplomatica!" Kellie realized no one was out here with them to refute this status. If saying yes could help them get out of the situation alive it was worth the lie. The next question was unexpected.

The lead officer was talking to Kellie asking a question she did not understand. He sounded suspicious about William. "What is he saying, William?"

"He wants to know why a diplomat would have a Puerto Rican with her if she was so important and if we were really cousins."

"Good question. Tell him you are my interpreter and we happen to be cousins. Not sure they will believe the cousin thing but tying that to diplomatic status may distract them from questioning that part of our story."

William translated the information. The officer then asked how they were cousins. William advised Kellie of this inquiry. Kellie realized the officers were paying attention.

"William, tell them you are my cousin from the marriage of my mother's brother who moved to Puerto Rico to raise his family. Also tell them that we are visiting another cousin twice removed, Damian Garrison."

"Kellie, if I try to describe that we will definitely be in trouble."

"Just do it, the more confusion the better. Make sure you say it all with conviction."

William translated the information. As he translated he could see that the officers were looking a bit uncertain. When he mentioned Damian's name there was a spark of recognition. William was afraid they would know Damian was a drug dealer and kill them on the spot. Mentioning his name was risky.

The lead officer started talking to his men. William could make out that they knew something about Damian. The officer turned to them and said he could take them to Damian's house as he was known to them. How he was known was the mystery.

William advised Kellie of this new information. "William, tell them that we appreciate their willingness to help, but we want to surprise him and if they could just point us in the right direction we would be out of their way and grateful."

William translated the information. He requested their help as to what road to take to the house on the coast that belonged to Damian. He showed them a crude map he had drawn from the banker's information where Andrew said the house would be.

The police hesitated, spoke among themselves and then pointed down the road. They advised them to take the left fork which would lead to a small dirt road on their left about six miles up. That road would lead them along the ocean road to his house.

"Muchas Gracias," replied William, "Muchas Gracias!"

"William let's go before they change their minds." Kellie grabbed William's arm and also thanked the officers in Spanish. "Gracias," she said, "Gracias."

Kellie and William got back in their car and began to leave when they heard shots fired in rapid succession.

•   •   •

The landing strip was situated five miles from the Vasquez family compound and three miles from the guest house where Damian was planning to go.

"Let's go ladies." Caleb was all too ready to get off the plane after their hard landing. He was tired and scared and hated coming to Damian's hideaway in Colombia. He knew this house was a safe house for the Vasquez family used mostly when some dealer working for them needed to see the family or take a break to avoid causing too much suspicion on their activities smuggling drugs for them . It was dangerous for Damian to bring anyone else there. He knew Jan and Marisa would never leave. Caleb just wanted to make sure he was able to leave when the time came.

"Caleb!" Damian barked. "Untie them. They would not do well if they try to run here."

Caleb untied Jan and Marisa's feet and cut the zip ties on their hands. As Jan rubbed her wrists she looked outside the plane window, nothing but dense brush and trees, no one in sight. Jan knew that being in Colombia was not a good thing; there was no way out.

Frank lowered the exit stairs. The humidity hit them like a ton of bricks, sticky hot and oppressive. "God I hate this weather," commented Damian. "It makes me irritable and short tempered." Damian let out a slight laugh and looked at Marisa and Jan.

"Caleb, get the Hummer, the key is on top of the driver's side rear tire."

Damian kept a Hummer in the underbrush covered by an old camouflage net. Caleb went to the underbrush about fifty yards from the plane. He pulled back the net mesh that could be mistaken for part of the overgrowth. Underneath was a black H2 and a small pickup truck with a filled fuel tank mounted on the bed. Caleb found the keys under the back tire of the H2 and drove it over to the plane.

"Frank, you stay here and refuel the plane the key to the fuel truck is in the glove compartment I want to be able to leave at a moment's notice. Get in girls." Damian commanded pointing his gun at their heads.

Marisa, Jan, and Damian got in the Hummer. Jan could tell Frank was not feeling so sure about being left behind, much less being in Colombia at all. As they drove away Jan could not help but think this trip would end in disaster.

•   •   •

As Kellie and William looked behind them they could see the military officers all laughing. The one who had looked the youngest and the most nervous was shooting his AK47 into the air as if he were celebrating. Kellie decided to keep driving unless they started firing on them directly.

"This is like the Old West, no law, no consequences," Kellie said. To her this was good and bad. Here she felt she could protect herself without answering to red tape but feared doing so would bring even more serious consequences or death. If they were killed, no one would know what happened to them.

Kellie and William drove in the direction they were told would lead to the coast and the house where Damian might be.

"William, when we get to the house we can't just barge in. We have to observe what is going on and be careful before we act. I don't want another shoot-out. The gun I got from Andrew has nine rounds left, no match for automatic weapons. Damian is sure to have security and plenty of firepower."

"I will do as you say, Kellie. I want the same thing you want, to rescue our loved ones." With that they both fell silent knowing the future for them and their loved ones was uncertain.

• • •

Jan and Marisa sat in the back while Caleb drove and Damian kept his eye and gun on them. As Jan looked out the darkened window of the H2 she could only see dirt road and jungle all around them. It did not take long to arrive at a remote dirt driveway blocked by an electric fence and gate. As the Hummer approached the gate it opened automatically. Damian drove the vehicle through the gate. It closed behind them leaving Jan with a sinking feeling in her stomach. It seemed as if they were driving for a while before they came to a stop in front of a beautiful mansion. In this part of Colombia, a house like this could only be bought by a drug lord. It was a hideaway, far from the city and main roads. Very few people probably even knew about the house or dared approach it.

"Damian, what do you want with us? Even if I told you everything I know what good would that do?" asked Marisa.

"Well my love, if I knew everything you told the government, and everything the government had on me from Jan's discovery file, I would be ahead of them in trying to arrest me or uncover my business activities with the Vasquez family. I would know who the informants were and have them eliminated before they could squeal."

"Listen to me Damian," Jan said. "The Vasquez family will find out what has happened and go after you for making such a mess."

"Shut up Counselor!" Damian replied with anger in his voice. "When I am done with you and Marisa, the Vasquez family will thank me. Do yourselves a favor and tell me what you know now and I will just put a bullet in the back of your heads instead of torturing you."

"Damian," Marisa said, "other people know about everything in my case. The Feds will still come for you."

"That may be true my love, but I will still be one step ahead of them by knowing what they know. I also know you lied to me to protect yourself and your stupid brother. I hate cleaning up other people's messes. You let your brother be careless and got yourself arrested. No one else in this organization has been arrested that was not killed for their mistakes. Surely you can see that I can't make an exception with you." Damian laughed out loud at his own amusing theory to justify killing Marisa and Jan.

Caleb let out an obliging nervous laugh. He was not much for the killing, but he was more afraid that Damian did not care who he killed if they got in his way, family or not. Caleb was just as afraid of Damian as anyone else.

As they drove up the driveway Jan could see four guards posted on the corners of the upstairs balcony that wrapped around the house. Along the driveway on each side was dense underbrush and trees.

Caleb drove up the long driveway to the circle drive in the front of the house. "Caleb, put the car in the garage and then join us in the house. Ladies, time to get out." Damian wanted everyone in the house before the guards asked any questions.

"Caleb, take the girls to the lower floor in the cell room. You will see a door on your left in the back of the kitchen. The stairs will lead you to a locked room. The key is on the side of the door. Put the ladies inside. Do you think you can do that without a problem?'

"Yes Damian," Caleb replied.

"Take your gun and shoot them if they give you any trouble. I will be along in a minute."

Caleb pushed Jan and Marisa, who was still limping, towards the front door of the house. "Move bitches."

Damian looked at the four guards and waived. He spoke to them in broken Spanish indicating he had some guests and did not want to be disturbed. He hoped they would think he was just in town for a break and had two good looking women with him for fun. He received a slight smile and wave from the guard at the west corner of the house. The others just stared at him, guns laid across their stomachs cradled by shoulder straps. The last thing Damian needed was to alert Santos, the Vasquez supervisor of death and destruction, or the Vasquez family themselves to his presence and problems. The guards were always at the Vasquez mansion to protect it from outsiders or other drug families.

As Caleb walked Jan and Marisa into the house Jan again tried to talk Caleb into helping them escape. "You know this is going to go badly for everyone. Get us all back to the plane and I can promise you no one will harm you."

Caleb did not respond as he heard Damian come into the house. "Get those girls down into the cell and lock the door!" he shouted.

Caleb pushed the girls to the back of the kitchen. Three steps down there was a metal door with a bolt lock. Caleb opened the door with a key he located on a hook next to the door. "Get in," he said as he opened the door.

As Jan and Marisa stepped down an additional light went on. "Welcome to your new home ladies," Caleb said.

Inside Jan could see two bunk beds in a room no bigger than eight by eight feet. There was a small toilet with no privacy and a sink.

"This is like being back in prison," Marisa said. "I can't take this, Damian please don't do this."

"Easy Marisa," Jan replied. "We will get out of here, somehow we will." Jan was not so sure of her own words. Things were getting desperate and they were nowhere near any friendly help.

Jan turned around as the door closed and the lock bolted shut. The light went out and she stood in the darkness. For the first time she felt alone, lost with no idea what do to.

"Marisa, let's get some sleep, we have had a rough trip and I can think better with some sleep. I will take the top bunk." Jan began to feel her way onto the top bunk.

"Jan," Marisa said, "I am so sorry for this mess. I am at my wit's end. I know Damian means to kill us." With that Marisa sat on the bottom bunk and started to cry. Jan listened but could give no comfort. She was tired and had nothing to offer. She had no idea what they were up against but knew it would be bad.

•   •   •

As DEA task force drug agents Thomas Chacon and Roberto Barto flew their law enforcement helicopter closer to Turbo they could see the small town by the river. Chacon was Roberto's partner in the DEA task force working out of Medellin. . They had been hooked up together by the agency because they both spoke Spanish. They were a part of the international effort between Colombia and the United States on stopping the flow of illegal narcotics to the states. Roberto had said little to Thomas on the flight except that they were looking for a remote place to land instead of the airport, something cut out of the jungle. It was common for agents to eventually find these makeshift landing strips if they flew low over the dense brush. A helicopter was the only way to fly low and slow.

"Roberto," Thomas asked through the flight headset they each wore to communicate over the loud noise of the helicopter, "what exactly are we looking for and what do we do when we find it?"

"I am going after a corrupt criminal defense attorney from the states who helped one of her clients escape and I believe they are with a major drug dealer from our country on his way to hook up with the Vasquez drug cartel near Turbo." Roberto did not want to alert Thomas to the fact that the attorney and maybe the client she helped were kidnapped. If there was any trouble Roberto wanted Thomas to believe everyone was suspect and therefore dangerous.

"When and if we find them we arrest them and ask questions later, right?" said Thomas.

"As long as there is no resistance, sure," replied Roberto. In his mind killing them all would do the United States and Colombia a favor. He intended to make sure there was some resistance.

• • •

Kellie and William were having trouble finding the road that led to the coast that would lead to the road to Damian's hideaway. They had driven up a couple of driveways that looked like roads but only led to empty lots with jungle overgrowth and trees. As they drove down one road they could see a clearing on the right with a plane sitting on a short grass runway. Kellie knew right away what it was, a local landing strip cut out of the jungle to help drug dealers get in and out of the area undetected.

"William," Kellie said, "See the landing strip and plane over there? What do you say we take a closer look? This landing strip is somewhere in the vicinity of the house we think Damian will be at. What if this is his plane and he is there with Jan and Marisa? We could head them off."

Kellie knew William was not happy about another detour. Kellie took the gun from behind her back and put it on her lap. She turned the Jeep down a grassy path off the road they were on and headed for the plane. As they got closer they could see a truck pulled up to the wing with a fuel line extended from a tank on the back of the truck to the plane fuel cap on the wing.

As they approached, the guy who was fueling the plane looked back at them with suspicion but did not stop what he was doing. Kellie drove the Jeep up beside the plane.

"Hey, you speak English?" asked Kellie.

"Yeah I speak English. Who are you and what do you want?"

"None of your business," replied William.

"We are looking for two friends." Kellie added. She described Marisa and Jan to Frank.-

Frank ignored Kellie and continued his business. He knew exactly who they were looking for.

William got out of the Jeep and walked up to Frank. "I know you, you fly for Damian, where is he?" William demanded.

"Where is who?" Frank replied trying to avoid giving out information on Damian.

"Damian you fool, you know who I am talking about."

Frank knew William, but was afraid to let him know what was going on.

Suddenly William grabbed Frank's pant belt pulling him off the fuel truck. They both fell to the ground the fuel pump pulling away from the wing and spilling fuel on the ground.

William began hitting Frank in the face screaming at him, "You bastard, tell me where my sister is!"

Frank was swinging wildly trying to hit William, but not making any contact. He rolled over under William trying to get him off of him. William shoved Frank's face into the dirt.

"Tell me where she is or I will break your neck!"

Kellie had no idea William was this intense, but she could see he was serious. Kellie reached for William's arm to pull him off of Frank.

"William this won't do us any good. Stop!"

Finally Kellie got William's attention enough for him to stop hitting Frank and sit on his back. William was out of breath.

"Let him up William!" Kellie said, "Let him up!"

William stood up and Frank pushed himself to his knees brushing the dirt from his face and mouth. As he did this Kellie quietly walked up and pushed the barrel of the Glock to the back of Frank's neck.

"Tell me what we want to know or I kill you here and leave your body for the buzzards." Kellie was tired of fooling around; they needed information and quickly. She held the gun steady in her hand. It was getting dark and they still had to find the house.

William moved to the side and let Kellie talk to Frank with the persuasion of a gun at his head. He noticed the fuel spill around them and went over to the truck to turn off the pump.

Kellie said impatiently. "Tell me where they are and what is going on! I am not in the mood for your games."

"Look, this is not my fight. I only do what I am told. I brought Damian here with Caleb and two women. I knew Marisa but not the other one. Damian called her Jan."

Kellie's heart sank. If they were too late she would never forgive herself.

"Where did they go?" she asked Frank.

"Damian goes to a house a few miles from here. They left about half hour ago."

"How far are we from the house?" Kellie asked.

"About five or ten minutes I think," replied Frank. "Go back to the road, turn left and go about three miles. The only dirt road you will see on the left will lead you to the house."

"William, let's go. I don't think we have much time."

"What should we do with him?" William asked.

"Leave him here. We will need him if we have to get out of here fast. Find some rope and tie him to the front plane wheel."

"Look," pleaded Frank, "I will wait here. Just don't tie me up; it's too dangerous!"

William found some rope in the plane. The inside of the plane was a mess but there was no sign of anyone. He brought the rope out.

"Get up," Kellie said pointing the gun at Frank's back. "Go sit by the nose wheel. Tie him up William, make it good."

"With pleasure," William replied. He tied Frank to the wheel gear despite Frank's protests and wove the rope around his legs tying the end to a portion of the wheel well out of reach. Frank could not move his hands up or down but could sit comfortably leaning against the front wheel.

"If all goes well Frank," Kellie said, "we will be back with two more passengers and we can all get out of here."

"Don't leave me. I swear I will wait. Take me with you, please."

Frank's plea went unanswered as Kellie and William drove off.

•   •   •

At the house, Damian had already had three shots of scotch to calm his nerves. Chivas Regal, always the choice of Colombians. "Have a drink Caleb."

Caleb poured himself a long shot of scotch and drank it down. He was in a foreign country, a drug kingpin's house, with his half-brother who would kill anyone who got in his way. He was now a part of a kidnapping over international boundaries. If he could he would drink the whole bottle of scotch and hope when he woke up this all would be a bad dream. If they got caught by the Vasquez family they would be tortured and killed. If the Colombian Federales found them they would be thrown in a Colombian jail for the rest of their lives. If DEA working with the Colombian police found them they would rot in a maximum prison in the U.S. None of these options was worth it.

Damian kept drinking. He was starting to slur his words. "Come on Caleb; drink up. The fun is just about to begin. Open the door to the girls' room; I want to see my girlfriend before I have to torture her. Get the syringes of sodium pentothal, the truth serum, in the refrigerator; it's show time."

Caleb did not like what was happening, but he had little choice but to comply. He retrieved two syringes from the refrigerator already filled with the truth serum. He turned to see Damian off balance with a nine millimeter in his left hand.

"Let's uh, let's go brother," Damian said in a slightly slurred but deliberate speech.

Caleb opened the door to the cell where Jan and Marissa were. The room was small and made of soundproof material so no one could hear anyone screaming. As the light went on, Jan opened her eyes but covered them with her hand to shield the strain on her eyes from the invading light. She had been asleep. She did not know for how long.

"Get up girls, Daddy's home," came Damian's drunken voice. "Caleb, stand guard at the door. I have business here."

Marisa had not been able to sleep. She was trying to think of something to distract Damian and Caleb. She knew he would kill them, or worse, torture them.

Damian walked over to the lower bunk and began caressing Marisa's breasts. She laid there looking at his face unsure of what to do next, he reeked of alcohol. Marisa realized she had fallen in love with a dream and not the reality of who Damian was. She had been so desperate to get out of her life of poverty and isolation that she never let herself see the real Damian.

"Damian, stop!" She slapped his hand off her breast. "If you love me let us go." Marisa was trying to think of something she could do or say that would save her and Jan from whatever Damian had planned for them.

Damian laughed and continued to paw at Marisa's breast, trying to kiss her.

"Come on baby, you know you love me. Give me some sex baby, before I have to ruin that beautiful body and mind. You know you like it." Damian was spitting out his words and unstable.

Jan jumped off the top bunk and landed on Damian's back. "Get off of her you creep!" Jan began whaling at Damian's head only to be pulled off by Caleb.

Damian got up but was not steady on his feet. He pulled his fist back to hit Jan, stopping in midair. Jan flinched, expecting a blow to her face.

"Good for you Jan, always trying to help others. I am not going to hit you just yet. I want you to be able to watch me get it on with Marisa while she tells me what she disclosed to the government before I do the same to you. Caleb, give me one of those syringes."

Caleb held out his left hand which held both syringes of the sodium pentothal. He was holding Jan around her chest and arms with his right arm. Damian took one of the syringes. "Caleb, hold that syringe to Jan's neck. If she moves, stick her. Stop struggling Jan, it won't do you any good."

Jan was suddenly terrified as a shot of sodium pentothal would incapacitate her and leave her unable to help herself or Marisa. Jan stopped struggling for fear she would cause Caleb to accidentally inject her.

"Damian please don't do this!" cried Marisa.

"Then talk to me Marisa. Tell me what I want to know."

"No Marisa, don't tell him anything, he will kill us anyway," Jan said.

"Hold her Caleb, I am going to give Marisa her medicine and then I am going to give it to her while you both watch, then I'll ask her my questions. I want to be in a good mood when I start getting the information I need. This will be fun. We might as well get some enjoyment for all the trouble you both have been. Caleb, you can have a go at Jan when I'm done here or Marisa for that matter. I don't care."

Damian laughed as he held the syringe to Marisa's neck in his left hand, the gun pointing at her from his right hand. Caleb was still holding Jan from behind with his syringe in his left hand against Jan's neck. Caleb was strong and could hold Jan back but he did not like what was about to happened.

"Stop Damian," Caleb said. "That's enough. You want to give them the shot, fine but I'm not going to watch you rape them."

"Well Caleb, look at you," Damian teased, "all chivalrous." Damian turned to Caleb with a smile and pointed the gun at Caleb's head. "Do you think I would hesitate to kill you, my half nitwit brother?"

As Damian turned his back on Marisa to talk to Caleb, she snatched the syringe from Damian's left hand and in one fluid motion stabbed him in the neck at the same time as she plunged the Pentothal liquid into his body. He pulled away before she could empty the syringe.

Damian's face registered surprise and shock as she only got half the serum in before he jerked back, but it was enough with the alcohol he had consumed to stop him. He turned to Marisa wanting to say something but could not feel his tongue. His head began to swim and in slow motion he saw the gun from his hand fall to the ground. Damian followed the path of the gun.

Caleb did not know what to do. "Don't move," he said, "or I will stick the syringe I am holding into Jan's neck."

"Caleb, get out of here while you can. You are not ruthless like Damian, he will kill you when he can get up. We are not staying, so put down the syringe; it's time we all leave," Marisa said.

Caleb stood there holding Jan and the syringe to her neck. Because Damian had been drinking that would make the effects of the drug even more intense. Maybe it was time for him to get away from Damian's influence. He was confused, but he also knew he could not kill anyone much less stick Jan with the needle. He was tired of the threats from Damian. This was too much.

"Enough," Caleb said to no one in particular. "Go," he said, "I will stay with him."

"Don't stay," Jan said. "Come with us."

Caleb wasn't sure what to do next. When Damian got up he would surely kill him. If he ran and Damian found him he would kill him. Either way Caleb was toast. He released Jan from his grasp.

"I don't want to leave him here. If the Vasquez family comes by and sees this mess they will kill him. As much as I hate him right now I can't let anyone harm him."

Jan was trying to think about their options now that Damian was on the floor disoriented.

"Alright," she said. "Let's make it look like we surprised you as well. Let me stick you with some of the sodium pentothal. That will put you out for a few minutes. I know you have been drinking but you should be about the same as Damian is now."

Jan could see Damian was struggling to get his wits about him but still did not have coordinated movements; it would not be long, however, before he would have the ability to get up.

Jan slowly took the syringe from Caleb's acquiescent hand and pushed a portion of the drug into his arm. Jan did not want to give him too much, just enough to weaken any possible resolve to change his mind and try to stop them.

She sprayed the rest of the liquid onto the floor. Caleb shook his head as if to say yes and quietly fell to his knees and then rolled on to his back, a smile of pleasure on his face as the warmth of the drug washed over him. It would not take long for the most immediate effect to war off.

Damian could see everyone, but could not comprehend what was going on. He could hear but not understand what they were saying. As he stared into the room he thought he saw Caleb fall to the ground next to him.

"Let's get out of here, Jan," Marisa said. "We don't have much time. Let's get back to the plane and try and to convince Frank to take us back to the states."

Jan went over to Damian and looked over him with disgust. "You pig." And with that she kicked him in his side. He winced but just stared up at her. She took their guns and gave one to Marisa. They would be of little use against the assault rifles the guards had outside.

"Jan I do not know how to use these firearms" Marisa lamented.

"Me either but I am not leaving them here", Jan replied.

• • •

Roberto and Thomas had been doing flyovers in a typical linear search pattern for an hour. "Come on Thomas, I know they are here somewhere."

"I'm trying," replied Thomas.

Roberto picked up the binoculars to look below. The jungle and surrounding area were dense, making seeing through the trees virtually impossible. He hated this part of his job, always trying to chase down the ghost-like dealers and their ever changing ways of doing business. It was getting late and they needed some luck to find the airfield.

"There!" Thomas shouted. He was pointing due east.

Roberto looked through the binoculars and saw the plane. As they approached he could see the small cut out airfield. "I see it," Roberto replied.

As Thomas maneuvered the helicopter closer, they could see there was enough room to land.

"Thomas set us down close to the plane." Roberto was giddy with anticipation of confronting and maybe killing some escapees and drug dealers. He said nothing about his feelings to Thomas.

Thomas set the chopper down gracefully about two hundred feet from the wing span of the plane. As quickly as he set down the chopper, Roberto was out the side door, gun drawn hoping for a conflict. His adrenalin was giving him a rush and rapid heartbeat. Adrenalin was Roberto's drug of choice. He ran in a ready position towards the plane. As he approached he could see Frank tied to the front wheel. Roberto approached cautiously. "DEA" he shouted. "Who are you and is anyone else in the plane?"

"I'm alone!" Frank shouted over the noise of the chopper, "Don't shoot!"

Roberto gave Thomas thumbs up to advise him to shut down the chopper. As Thomas did this he kept his eyes on Roberto.

Roberto moved cautiously closer to Frank his gun still pointing at him.

"What are you doing here?" Roberto asked.

"It's a long story. Cut me loose and I will tell you."

"No, tell me now, and then I will decide if I want to untie you."

"I took some passengers here from the U.S. for a little R&R. I was going to join them when I tied down the plane but someone else showed up and tied me up. They wanted to know who I transported and where they were." Frank was trying to lie just enough to keep himself out of trouble with the Feds.

At this point Thomas joined them. "So what's the story Roberto, big drug pilot?"

"According to Frank, he brought some tourists here for a vacation." Roberto knew the story was not true. There is no tourist trade near Turbo, Colombia. To motivate the truth, Roberto suddenly kicked Frank in his rib cage. Frank screamed in pain. Roberto kicked him again.

"I would like the truth, you dirt bag. Did you think we were stupid?"

"Ok, Ok," Frank cried. I was hired by a guy named Damian. He came here with two girls and his bodyguard." Roberto kicked him again. "For God's sake stop!" he moaned out of breath.

"Easy Roberto," Thomas said. "We need him to talk."

"Back off Thomas, this scum knows more than he is telling. So talk! Where did they go?"

"They went to a house on the coast up a dirt road. They said they were coming back."

"Who are they? Tell me about everyone who came by," Roberto demanded.

"There were the passengers and another guy and girl with a gun who came by after everyone else left. The guy's name was William; the woman had a gun. He tied me up and said they would be back with passengers to get out of here. Now untie me."

"No, we need to be sure you stay here. Where are the keys to the fuel truck?" Roberto demanded.

"In the truck," replied Frank. "Please don't leave me here!"

Thomas and Roberto were already getting into the truck when Thomas said: "We need to take him with us to show us where to go."

"You be responsible for him," Roberto acquiesced. "If he gets in the way I will kill him."

Roberto did not want anyone else to get in the way of his ultimate plans but he knew they would find the house faster with Frank than without him.

Thomas was not comfortable with Roberto's bravado, but would not risk their mission either. He went over to Frank and with a swift motion from his sharp hunting knife, cut the zip ties on Frank's legs and hands.

"Thanks," Frank said.

"Don't thank me yet Frank, my partner would rather kill you. Don't give him an excuse to do it."

Frank got up slowly, holding his side. He was sure a rib was broken, but he was not about to stay there as darkness fell and fuel covered the ground around them.

All three got in the front cab of the truck with Frank in the middle for security purposes. "Which way?" asked Thomas.

"Out this way and turn left at the dirt road." He pointed in the direction of where everyone went.

•   •   •

Jan and Marisa started to leave Damian's hideaway. As they were leaving the kitchen area, Jan stopped.

"What?" Marisa asked.

Jan knew they were still in serious danger. They still had to get past the outside armed guards.

"We have to find a way to sneak out of here before Damian and Caleb can get up. We have to get past the guards outside without being shot." It was also getting dark outside and they needed to see where they were going without being seen.

"Marisa," Jan said, "It's getting late; let's see if we can find a flashlight before we go."

They both went to the kitchen and began frantically looking for a flashlight. While Jan checked the kitchen drawers Marisa checked the pantry. There were two flashlights hanging on the inside of the pantry door. One worked, but the other was too dim from low battery power to be of any use.

"What do we do about the guards outside?" Marisa asked.

"Good question," replied Jan. "We could sneak out the garage into the woods, but that would leave us to guess where the main road was and how to get there."

"If we go outside, the guards will see us and know something is wrong," Marisa said. "We have little choice."

Marisa and Jan looked around the lower level of the house to find a door to the garage. Inside was the H2. They looked for the keys in the ignition and the visor but could not find them. They left the guns they got from Damian and Caleb in the H2. They would be of no use against the automatic weapons the guards had and shooting back would only slow them down. Neither of them knew enough about shooting or killing to be worth the risk. Running was there only choice.

"Should we go back in and try to find the keys?" Marisa asked.

"No, I'm afraid that Damian will soon be able to move and will try to kill us," replied Jan. "We will have to take our chances outside on foot. Marisa, in the rush to get out of there I did not think to lock the cell door when we left to keep Caleb and Damian in."

"Too late now Jan, too risky to go back; we have to get out of here," Marisa replied.

They eased their way along the garage wall to get around the Hummer. When they got to the open garage door they peered around the corners to see if anyone was nearby. No one was watching the area, but they could see one of the guards on the upstairs wrap-around balcony walking to the other side of the house.

"You go first," Jan said to Marisa. "Can you do this with your bad ankle?"

"I'm okay for now. It hurts a little, but I can run with a limp. I will have to watch where I'm going to avoid injuring it more, but I don't want to slow us down."

Marisa ran with a slight limp across the driveway from the garage to the woods and immediately ducked behind a tree. The guard had turned around and was moving towards them walking the back of the balcony like a cat on the prowl. Marisa could see the guard better than Jan. If Jan ran out now they would be seen. Marisa held up her hand to stop Jan from moving. Jan did not see her and ran across the driveway. As she did, the sound of her footsteps alerted the guard.

"Stop!" the guard shouted in English. He shot off two warning shots. "Stop!"

Jan never hesitated. She ran into the woods where Marisa had run. Shots rang out and splintered the trees around them. They were both moving low to the ground in a gulch area that followed the driveway down to the road while bullets were whizzing by.

The guards' gunfire alerted the others and they all came to the front of the property. Speaking in Spanish they conversed rapidly. Two of the guards went inside the house while the other two kept firing in the location they thought Marisa and Jan were going. Fortunately the gully and dusk shadows kept the guards from seeing them clearly. They were spraying the trees wildly with machine gun fire hoping to hit them.

Jan's heart was pounding in her chest. It was hard to see the ground and she was afraid she would fall on broken trees or trip over their roots. She did not want to be one of those stupid girls in movies who always tripped so the bad guys could catch them. She knew this was no movie, if they were captured now it would be the end.

"I am not ready to die!" Jan screamed. "Run Marisa, run!"

• • •

As the two guards that entered the house went downstairs, they began to search the house. They came upon the room where Damian and Caleb were. As they entered they could see both of them struggling to get up.

"Senior Damian, are you alright, what happened?" one guard asked. Though Spanish was the guard's native language he could speak some broken English.

Damian was groggy but he slurred his words to tell the guard the girls had escaped. "Gooooo!" is all he could say clearly as he pointed out the door.

• • •

Kellie and William had driven, according to the odometer, a little over three miles. It was dusk, so Kellie put the headlights on as the streets reflected dark shadows from the trees and thick foliage. Suddenly William shouted pointing behind them, "Kellie there was a dirt road on your left. You just missed it; turn around!"

Kellie braked hard and skidded to a stop. She quickly turned around and headed down the dirt road. They came to a gate about half mile up the road and stopped.

"Ram the gate, Kellie," William said. "Hurry!"

Kellie backed up about five car lengths and floored the Jeep. Ducking their heads, the gate gave way at the center without falling off its hinges.

• • •

Jan and Marisa were running down the hill towards the bottom of the driveway. It would take them a long time to get to the plane, but that was their only hope to get out of there. It was dark and hard to see but turning on the flashlight would let the guards know where they were. They had to stay hidden but were having trouble seeing and needed help.

"Marisa, how is the ankle?"

"Okay for now. I don't want to slow us down. Keep running Jan. I will stay right behind you."

Jan knew they could not keep up a running pace for the two or three miles they would have to travel to get to the plane before someone caught up to them or killed them. Marisa was slowing down and falling behind. Jan thought if she could make it to the main road maybe she could get some help before anyone caught up to them.

Up ahead, Jan could see some headlights, but could not see who it was or what kind of vehicle. She was afraid to step out of the thick underbrush for fear it was more of Damian's men. She let the vehicle pass identifying it as a gold color Jeep Cherokee. She could not see through the dark windows who was inside.

Out of breath Jan stopped to let Marisa catch up.

"Who was that in the car?" Marisa asked.

"I don't know but we can't be sure it was not more guards with guns. We have to keep going."

•   •   •

Kellie drove up the driveway with the headlights off. At the top of a small hill perched the yellow house. It was bigger than any house in the area and clearly out of place in this part of Colombia. As Kellie and William drove closer, they slowed down. They were about five hundred feet from the house when Kellie heard gunfire.

"We should stop here William, do you hear the gunfire? Sounds like automatic weapons. I will go up on foot to see what is going on, you stay here. I have a gun and I don't want you to get killed."

"No problem," William replied. "I'll turn the car around; keep it running and ready to leave if there is trouble. I don't have your training so I am not sure what help I would be facing those guns."

Kellie pulled the Jeep over to the side out of the line of sight of the house, got out, and began moving quietly along the left side of the long curved driveway close to the woods. As she got closer she could hear more gunfire and shouting. Slowly she crept up to a spot where she could see the front of the house from behind a tree without exposing herself. She could see the guards with guns; they were pointing them at the tree line. Every now and then a series of shots would ring out as if the guards had seen something and were trying to hit whatever it was. Kellie could see they were not aiming at her, at least not yet. There appeared to be four guards all together, two shooting at the tree line and two looking for someone or something in the brush near the house. Suddenly two other men came stumbling out of the front door of the house. She could hear some of what was being said.

"Go look in the woods for them. Find them!"

The shouts were coming from a man being supported by another man as they came out of the house. Kellie could not tell if one of them was Damian. She realized they had to be looking for Jan and Marisa. Good for them, Kellie thought, they have escaped, but where are they?

As Kellie observed the chaos, two of Damian's weapon-toting henchmen were headed down the driveway for the woods, right where she was hiding. A third one was talking on a cell phone, another firing into the trees across the driveway from the house. Her Glock was no match for their automatic weapons. Kellie knew she had to find Marisa and Jan before the men found any of them.

•   •   •

Thomas, Frank, and Roberto were close to the road to Damian's house.

"Look Thomas," Roberto said. "We need to approach carefully but shoot first and ask questions later."

Frank was scared, he knew that Damian had a lot of fire power at the house and there were always guards helping out. He began to think staying tied up at the plane might have been safer.

"There," Frank said as he pointed to a dirt road. "Turn here."

Thomas turned the truck left and started up the road. They soon came upon Damian's driveway and the broken open gate. As they started up the driveway they saw a gold color Jeep Cherokee, lights out, sitting to the side, facing down the driveway towards the road they were driving up. Someone was in the Jeep.

"That's the place" Frank said. "Man you better not go up there. Damian will kill anyone he does not expect or know."

"Who do we have here?" Thomas inquired as they approached the Jeep.

"Stop the car, Thomas," ordered Roberto.

As the car started to slow down Roberto was out of it in a flash, gun drawn, crouched low. Whoever was in the gold Jeep Cherokee had ducked down trying not to be seen.

"DEA" shouted Roberto. "Hands up and get out of the car!"

No response came from the car. "DEA, I will shoot you, get out of the car with your hands up!"

William lay frozen below the steering wheel across the center console. He was afraid to answer for fear of getting caught which could result in everyone getting killed. He was also afraid of getting shot. He did not know what to do.

As William began to raise his hands to surrender he heard loud gunfire. He thought the DEA guy was shooting at him. "Stop, I give up, don't shoot!"

The gunfire became even more rapid. Pure instinct told William he was better off ducking back down. He could not see anything but headlight reflections.

"Thomas, get out of here. Someone is shooting at us up the road!" yelled Roberto.

Roberto jumped back in the fuel truck. Thomas floored the truck up the driveway, braked hard and spun around sliding off the driveway into a ditch almost turning as the half full fuel tank attached to the bed of the truck shifted. They all scrambled out of the truck and ducked behind it. On the angle the truck landed in was harder for anyone shoot at them. Frank trembling, agents' guns drawn, they all laid there listening. The gunfire was close, but did not seem to be aimed at them.

•　　•　　•

Marisa and Jan were close to the end of the driveway. They would soon be down to the road that led to the main road back to the plane.

"How are you doing Marisa?" Jan asked.

"Not great but I am still moving. The gunfire is motivation enough to keep going."

Jan could hear the gunfire but it seemed more random and not as close to where they were. She stopped again to wait for Marisa to catch up.

Kellie could see men in the garage getting into a Hummer while others started down the driveway on foot, parallel to the woods, looking with flash-lights into the dense tree line. Kellie could not stay where she was; she had to go back to the car where William was waiting. As she turned into the woods to keep her cover she heard some voices, she stopped to listen.

She heard someone say: "Are you all right?" It sounded like the voices were past her down the drive headed towards William. It sounded like Jan's voice, or maybe she just wanted it to be her, and it really was someone else or someone with bad intentions. She was afraid to speak up and yell for fear of giving herself away. She waited a little longer. She could hear footsteps in the woods and shouting coming at her from the house. She could not wait any longer. Kellie could not see anything but she knew she had to take a risk to see if the voice she heard was Jan.

"Jan?" she said softly. "Jan?" No answer.

"There, there is one of them!" came a voice in broken English.

Kellie heard the gunfire and in a split second hit the ground just in time to hear the whiz of bullets go over her head and into some trees. She decided she had no choice but to fire back, if for nothing else than to make them take cover and give her a few more seconds to get away. She sent three shots out in the direction of her assailant's flashlights. She knew she had to get to William and out of there before they were killed. If she were dead, she would be no help to Jan and Marisa. Besides, Jan would never forgive her for leaving her alone; she loved Jan so much that she was determined to find her.

Kellie went down the driveway in a crouched run along the edge of the trees until she reached the Jeep. She went to get in the passenger side which was on the opposite side of the driveway near the ditch when she saw something from her left peripheral vision. She turned, gun pointed.

"DEA!" shouted Roberto. "Put down your weapon."

Kellie was in no mood to negotiate with the DEA and try to explain what was going on. "No you put your weapon down. I'm in a hurry!" Kellie replied pointing the Glock at the agent.

Just as she said these words more gunfire erupted around them. Roberto once again hit the ground and rolled to find cover behind the fuel truck. William could hear what was going on but was afraid to look behind him. He was crouched down in the driver's seat, lights off, engine running ready to leave.

"William, get us out of here!" Kellie shouted as she opened the passenger door and got in.

"With pleasure," he replied. "What about Jan and Marisa?"

"They are out here somewhere but if we stay here we will be killed either by the DEA or Damian and his posse."

Roberto was getting frustrated. "This is ridiculous!" he complained. "I'm tired of this crap, let's start shooting back."

"No Roberto, we are behind a bomb for God's sake. If we get a bullet in the right place this whole truck will explode."

"It will take more than a bullet in the fuel tank. It is not metal and a spark would have to ignite it."

"I am not willing to take that chance!" Thomas shouted. .

Roberto started shooting in the direction of the gunfire. They could see flashlights and the headlights of a big vehicle. As Roberto fired the flashlights and headlights went out.

Kellie and William started to drive down the dirt road to go back to the main road heading to the plane. "Who was that DEA guy?" Kellie asked.

"I have no idea," William replied, "He was trying to get me out of the car when the gunfire started. I was about to give up when you showed up. I think he was going to shoot me."

"How would they even know what was going on here?" Kellie was concerned that DEA had shown up at all. How would they have found out about them? Or, was it just a coincidence that they were there? Was there an undercover operation going on here? Kellie pondered her own questions. Someone knows what is going on and has sent help or harm. From what was already happening it was not easy to tell.

•   •   •

Jan and Marisa could hear the commotion and gunfire all around them but the bullets seemed to be going in a different direction now.

"I think we are about at the end of the driveway near the main road," Jan whispered to Marisa. "We need to stay in the woods to avoid being seen."

"Jan, when we were in the woods running I thought I heard someone," Marisa said.

"Probably Damian and his henchman, come on Marisa we have to keep going."

Jan and Marisa came to the end of the driveway at the gate which lead to the dirt road. As she approached the gate she could hear a car coming and whispered to Marisa, "Get down; someone is coming."

Jan could see what looked like a gold Jeep coming towards them. She had not seen that car at the house but had no idea if this car was friend or foe. Who was in the Jeep and what did they want? Should she take a risk and flag them down? These thoughts escalated her fears but she knew they had little choice at this point, there was no way they could get to the plane before they were discovered and in the dark they would have difficulty finding their way. Walking or running as far as they had come with Marisa's bad leg already took too long. Getting to the plane would be even more difficult.

"Marisa," Jan said, "I am going to flag this car down. You stay put. No matter what happens to me don't give yourself away."

"Are you sure that is a good idea, Jan? What if it is Damian or his men; we will end up right back where we started."

Without responding, Jan pushed her way out of the woods and thickets stepping to the side of the road. As the Jeep approached, Jan hesitated. She could not see clearly. Suddenly the lights on the car were shining in her eyes. She could not see anything. She heard the car skid on the gravel to a stop right in front of her. All she could think of was a deer in headlights, she was frozen with fear that it was Damian or his guards.

Kellie jumped out of the car before it stopped. "Jan!" Kellie screamed— "Jan!" Kellie ran around the front of the vehicle sweeping Jan into her arms. "Oh God baby I thought I would never find you!"

"Oh my God! Kellie, how did you find us? I can't believe it is you! How did you find us!" Jan began to cry realizing how much fear and apprehension had been building up. She held on to Kellie burying her face in her neck. Jan was trembling.

"It's going to be okay baby," Kellie said as calmly as possible. "We have to get out of here. Tell me, where is Marisa?"

"Here I am," came Marisa's voice as she came out of the underbrush.

William could not believe his eyes. He put the car in park and got out. "Marisa!" William shouted.

Marisa was even more stunned than William. She could not move, she had no idea her brother was still alive. She could not speak.

William came to her and put his arms around her. They looked into each other's eyes and both began to cry. The joy of seeing William alive was too much for words.

· · ·

Damian was in the passenger seat as Caleb drove down the driveway as shots were being fired into the woods by two of his running down the driveway. Damian found the guns the girls left in the Hummer. Damian was getting angrier by the minute as he tried to regain his senses. Caleb was hoping Damian would believe him when he told him that the girls had overpowered him as well.

As Caleb drove down the road, slightly weaving, Damian pulled an UZI from under his seat. He gave one of the handguns to Caleb. "They could not have gotten far on foot."

Two of the other guards retrieved another car, an old Honda Accord, sitting in the drive way and had already headed down towards the main road trying to head the girls off ahead of the Hummer. Damian could hear shots being fired coming from both directions. Halfway down the driveway he could see his men were stopped and crouching behind their car doors firing back at someone ahead of them in the ditch.

As Damian pulled up behind the Honda he could see it was the fuel truck sitting in the ditch. He was having trouble understanding why bullets were hitting the front of the H2 and coming from the behind the truck at the same time. Damian was now glad he had bullet proof glass put in the Hummer.

"Caleb, get out there and help. Start firing at the truck in the ditch."

Caleb hesitated. He got behind the door of the H2. Shots were being fired from everywhere. Caleb was still not clearheaded and had no idea what or who he was shooting at.

"Thomas, how many rounds do you have left?" Roberto asked as bullets flew by hitting the truck and the trees around them.

"I have about five in my gun and two clips," he replied. "How about you?"

"I have a backup nine millimeter with one clip but only five rounds left in my Glock."

Roberto started barking out orders. "We have to get out of here, we are outgunned. Frank, we need you to drive." Frank was still crouched behind the truck. "We will cover you. Get in the driver's seat now!"

"Are you kidding? I could get killed. The bullets could hit the fuel tank on the truck."

Roberto turned to Frank and said: "Get in the truck and drive or I will kill you myself. We will cover you."

Thomas and Roberto stood up and started shooting while Frank got in the passenger side of the truck and slid over to the driver's side. "Get in Thomas!" Roberto yelled.

Thomas got in and moved to the center of the front seat with Roberto jumping in next to him. "Go Frank, go!"

Frank stepped on the gas as a hail of bullets slammed into the truck and shattered the back window. He was having trouble getting the truck out of the ditch, the back tire spinning in the mud.

"Rock the truck!" shouted Thomas.

Frank frantically shifted the gears to move the truck forward and back trying to free it. Bullets were hitting the truck everywhere. Thomas was shooting out the broken back window while Roberto continued shooting, leaning out of the passenger window. At least this gave them some time as it forced the other shooters to take cover before returning fire again.

• • •

Jan, Kellie, Marisa, and William could hear the gun fire just up the drive but Marisa held on to her brother not believing he was alive after all this time.

"William what happened to you?" Marisa asked tears running down her face.

"It's a long story Marisa, but right now there is not enough have time to tell it."

"Honey," Kellie said in Jan's ear, "we have to get out of here."

Jan did not want to let go of Kellie but knew they needed to leave. They were not out of danger yet.

"Everyone, please get in the car quickly!" Kellie shouted.

• • •

Frank had finally gotten the truck free. Frank, Thomas, and Roberto started back down the driveway to the dirt road trying to catch up to Kellie and William. They could see the Jeep ahead of them. Roberto started shooting out the window towards their car. He wanted to stop them one way or another. They were the key to his success and gave him some negotiating power to get out of this dangerous situation. He was trying to hit the car tires to stop them while gunfire was still coming from behind them and Thomas was still shooting at the cars that were following them.

As Kellie, Jan, Marisa, and William were all getting into the Jeep the gunfire caught up to them. Bullets were hitting the Jeep and the back window shattered. Suddenly Jan fell to the ground just before she was able to get into the back seat of the Jeep. Kellie saw Jan fall.

"No!" Kellie screamed. She could see blood coming from Jan's right temple area. "Oh please God! Not now!" Kellie ran to where Jan fell and with her adrenaline pumping picked her up in her arms and cradled her into the back seat.

Marisa jumped into the back seat next to where Kellie had laid Jan. "Marisa, grab something to press against the wound!" Kellie shouted. "William, get us out of here!"

Kellie started shooting out the passenger side window hoping to slow down whoever was shooting at them. She got in the car after firing three rounds. William took off, this time spinning his wheels in the gravel before the tires caught the road.

William was flying down the road with Thomas, Roberto and Frank closing in behind them in the fuel truck. Damian, Caleb and his guards were closing in on all of them in the Hummer and Honda driven by two of the guards from the house.

Kellie pulled her gun in from shooting out the window and turned to Marisa trying not to panic. "Is Jan okay? Where is the bleeding coming from?"

"I can't tell Kellie. She needs a doctor or a hospital!"

Kellie thought Jan was either unconscious or worse, dead. Marisa was wearing a camisole tank top under her blouse. She took that off, put her shirt back on and pressed the camisole against Jan's head. Immediately it became soaked in Jan's blood.

"I can't stop the bleeding. We have to find a doctor!" Marisa cried.

"There is nothing around here," William said. "Believe me, we have been to the town. If we go back we might be killed. We have to get out of here and the plane is our only hope."

"Frank should be at the plane, we can make him fly us out of here," said Kellie. She had no idea Frank was no longer tied up at the plane.

Kellie was devastated. Losing Jan would destroy her. She could not face the future without her even think of how to tell her family what happened. They had to do something.

•   •   •

William came to the main road and took a hard right. As he did he could see the headlights of the fuel truck just behind them.

"Kellie! Kellie!" William shouted. "Kellie, I need you with me!"

Kellie had just been staring at Jan watching the blood seep from her forehead soaking into Marisa's camisole. "Sorry William, I can't lose Jan."

"Look we are not going to lose her; we just have to get out of here!" William was shouting at Kellie to get her to focus on their situation and not Jan. If she did not do so, they would all die.

Kellie came back to her senses. What was important now was to get them all to safety. "Let's go back to the plane. Step on it William."

William floored the Jeep. He was flying down the main road going 80 miles per hour. In the rear view mirror he could see the truck turn onto the road followed by the H2. The fuel truck was about a half mile behind but they would catch up as soon as they reached the plane.

Marisa was holding an unconscious Jan bleeding badly from a head wound but there was no sign of a bullet entry. She must have been hit by a ricochet bullet, Marisa thought. It was hard to see how serious it was due to all the blood. Marisa started rubbing Jan's cheeks lightly slapping them. "Jan wake up, come on girl wake up; we need you here!"

Jan moaned but did not open her eyes. "Come on Jan," Marisa said. "Wake up!"

Kellie looked back. "Come on Jan!" she said. Kellie reached over and squeezed Jan's hand. "Honey, I'm here, I will not let anything happen to you. Come on baby, let me know you are here with us."

Jan could hear Marisa and Kellie but her mind was not responding though she thought she was trying to say something. She could feel Kellie's hand and squeezed back. "I'm here my love, I'm here." Nothing came out. Jan's head hurt so much she just wanted to go to sleep.

"She squeezed my hand!" Kellie said. "At least I know she is alive in there."

The blood from Jan's wound was all over Marisa and the car. Marisa continued to press on the wound trying to stop the bleeding.

"Keep the pressure on the wound, Marisa," Kellie said.

"I'm trying Kellie," Marisa replied. "I love Jan too and I would do anything for her."

"Look," William said. "There's the plane but look what is next to it."

As they approached the runway where the plane had been they could see the helicopter the DEA had flown in on.

"Sweet Jesus!" cried William, "The hell with Frank, I can fly that," he said pointing to the helicopter.

William was excited, finally he could be of some use. He drove the car up to the helicopter. It could hold four, but it would be tight and the lift might be a struggle.

"I'm not sure we can all get in this thing," explained William.

Kellie looked around for Frank. "Where is Frank?" she said to the others. "He's gone."

Kellie and William got out of the Jeep. Marisa was still holding Jan's head. They could hear the fuel truck coming up on them.

As the truck pulled up Roberto and Thomas jumped out and stood behind the doors with their guns drawn.

"All of you stop right there!" shouted Roberto. "Put your hands up and get on your knees, DEA!"

Kellie turned to them and said: "Shut up, both of you. I am not in the mood to listen to you two act out your law enforcement fantasies. We are all in trouble in case you didn't notice!" As she said this she pointed behind them. As Thomas turned he could see the H2 closing in on them fast.

"I don't care about them. I will shoot you and then them if you do not do what I say!" shouted Roberto.

"Look Roberto," Thomas said, "she's right, we are all about to get killed. I do not think these guys behind us care if we are DEA; in fact that is more likely to get us killed. Let them go and let's get out of here now, we do not have enough firepower to win this war!"

"No!" shouted Roberto, "This is my moment, I am going to get rid of some escaped convicts and their aiders and abettors and then get rid of some drug dealers. No one will want to know what happened, they will thank us."

"Roberto!" Thomas screamed, "You are crazy, it is us that will be killed! Even if we kill the escapees we cannot match the H2 group firepower!"

Kellie knew they were wasting time. "Hey stupid DEA, I was once an FBI agent and know your cowboy type. You kill us and you will have one hell of an investigation into why you killed innocent people. That's if you don't get killed yourself. We are leaving, I have a wounded friend in the car, and you cannot stop us." Kellie could only pray the agents would not shoot them all.

Kellie went to the back door of the Jeep to help Marisa get Jan out of the car. Jan was still bleeding but not as much and she seemed to be gaining some consciousness. She was at least starting to move. Kellie found a rag in the console of the Jeep. "Here put this on her head. Tie it tightly around the wound. It's not perfect but may help keep the pressure on to help stop the bleeding. . ."

"Let's go everyone!" yelled William. He was walking to the chopper when Roberto went after him.

Kellie raised her gun. "Stop right there Mr. DEA or I will shoot you!"

Roberto could not believe his ears. He hesitated knowing his gun was pointed at William and that he could not turn fast enough to shoot Kellie. He was exposed when he moved away from the cover of the truck.

"Thomas," Roberto said, "Shoot her, shoot her!"

Thomas saw what was going on, but also saw the H2 only a few hundred yards away. It had slowed down but was still coming at them.

"Roberto, this is crazy, these people are not the bad guys: the ones about to be here are."

Suddenly a series of shots rang out, everyone ducked. Roberto was not fast enough and took a bullet in the back. He fell where he stood. The next rain of bullets hit the truck and this time the fuel tank caught on fire.

Frank jumped out of the truck just as the truck blew up. The explosion rocked the ground and catapulted the truck, over Roberto's body into the helicopter which also exploded on impact. Everyone fell to the ground covering their heads from flying helicopter blades and debris. The Hummer stopped to avoid getting hit by chopper debris. Fortunately nothing seemed to have hit the plane.

Kellie's ears were ringing as she slowly got up. She could see that Thomas was also having a hard time getting up. Kellie yelled at him not knowing his name.

"Hey agent, you okay?"

"I think so," Thomas replied. Thomas got up and saw Roberto on the ground. He stumbled over to his body.

"There is nothing we can do for him!" shouted Thomas realizing they were still in danger. "We need to get out of here, all of us. The copter is toast, we need to get on that plane now!"

"Look Thomas, we can't afford to take you with us if you are going to turn us in or kill us later," Kellie said.

"I am not like Roberto, the real bad guys are behind us and will kill all of us. I promise you have nothing to fear from me." Thomas was scared and for now had no intentions of being left behind even if he had to lie.

"As a former agent, I believe you," Kellie said. "We should take Roberto's body out with us. Help me get him into the plane."

Kellie ran back to Jan to see if she was hurt. Jan moaned and was trying to get up.

"Marisa, you okay?"

"Yes, William is here with me; we are both okay."

"Marisa can you help Jan into the plane?" yelled Kellie.

"Yes, go help the agent."

Kellie and Thomas picked Roberto's body up by his arms and dragged him to the plane. They stopped at the stairs to let Frank get in the cockpit with William. They had no time for a preflight check and started the engines of the six passenger private prop jet. Frank was yelling to the others to hurry.

Kellie could see that the explosion helped keep Damian and his crew away for the moment but as soon as the flames allowed, they would be on them like white on rice. It was hard to tell if there was any damage to the plane from the debris but it was dark and there was no way to do a detailed inspection. The plane's wings and rudder were attached and the engine worked. For now that would have to do.

Marisa was having trouble getting Jan to walk onto the plane and she was too heavy for Marisa to carry alone.

"Thomas!" Kellie said letting go of Roberto, "leave Roberto and help me get my partner into the jet, she was wounded by the gunfire!"

Thomas could see Jan's makeshift bandage was blood-soaked. He dropped Roberto's torso and helped Kellie pick Jan up, each holding one side of her body under her arms. They lifted her up the stairs turning sideways to fit through the jet door. They gently sat Jan down in one of the seats. Marisa was up the stairs and sat next to Jan pressing the shirt bandage tightly on her head and buckled them both in.

"We have to get out of here!" screamed Frank from the cockpit. "Damian is just on the other side of the flames. He's shooting at us!"

"We have to get Roberto's body!" Thomas claimed.

"No time," said Kellie. She shut the door to the plane over Thomas' protests. "Go Frank, Go!

"Stop!" shouted Thomas. "We can't leave him!"

It was too late; they all could hear the guns firing and bullets pelting the plane. Frank was already taking off in a hail of bullets. Thomas had no time to buckle up. As they were taking off Thomas fell to the floor sliding to the back of the plane. Jan and Marisa were belted in and holding on. Kellie grabbed a seat and held on just as they took off.

Frank got them off the ground but Damian was running the H2 right under them along the grass runway. From under the plane, even though Frank had the plane in a steep climb, Damian was firing everything he had. Frank made it past the end of the runway forcing Damian to stop but he and his guards continued to fire multiple rounds at the fleeing plane.

Suddenly one of the two engines on the jet burst into flames. A built-in engine fire extinguisher put out the flames, but the plane was already crippled. Frank was struggling to keep the plane level without losing the little altitude they had gained. He had been able to get them to about two thousand feet but was struggling to maintain his climb.

"William, look out the plane at the wing!" Frank shouted, "What do you see?"

"Looks bad," replied William. "The engine is burned badly. I can also see bullet holes in the wing and fuel leaking."

"We can fly at this level with one engine but the fuel leak will limit our distance." Frank was contemplating what it would be like to crash into a remote area of Colombia, never to be found. He had to clear his head and get them somewhere populated. His Naval training started to kick in.

"We can't go very far with this damage, we will never make Medellin. William pull out those charts and find me the coordinates for the closest airport."

"Frank, we can't go there," William said.

"Why not? It is right here pointing to the Turbo airfield. We are up and now we can go down in minutes ."

"We can't go back to Turbo, we already had a run in there and the authorities might be looking for us." William revealed this information to Frank in hopes he would cooperate and find somewhere else to land.

"What about Apartado" offered William pointing to the town on the map Frank was looking at.

Kellie got up once the plane leveled off at twenty-five hundred feet, all the altitude Frank could muster, and went over to Jan and Marisa. "You okay, Marisa?"

"Yes, I'm fine. Jan is trying to wake up but is having trouble. I think she was grazed, I can't find a bullet hole in her head but she probably has a bad concussion and will need stitches."

Kellie sat down, worried and tired from all the stress and adrenaline pumping through her body.

"You okay?" Thomas asked Kellie. "My name is Thomas." He put out his hand.

Kellie had not realized it but Thomas did not know them.

"My name is Kellie," she shook Thomas's hand. "This is Marisa and my partner Jan. Frank you already know and with up front with Frank is William, Marisa's brother."

"Nice to meet all of you," Thomas replied. "Sorry it had to be under these circumstances. Why was Roberto so anxious to kill you guys? And what is this escape thing he kept talking about?"

Kellie did not want to disclose too much but wanted to know what Thomas had been told by Roberto.

"What do you know so far?" Kellie asked him.

"Roberto was not too clear about the mission. He said he was chasing an escaped convict from America and her lawyer who assisted in the escape. He also said there was a big drug dealer involved and that we could score big if we could find the escaped convict. The drug markets in the U.S. are vast, so it is hard for us to keep up with the problem. The dealers here have a lot of money and power. Our judges and prosecutors get killed every day when trying to charge and convict the big drug families. Sending the criminals back to the U.S. is safer for us. I thought that was his plan."

"It is true Marisa escaped from prison," Kellie began, "but she was not assisted by her attorney." Kellie was not about to tell Thomas Jan was Marisa's attorney.

"Then who did help her?" inquired Thomas.

"Let's just say she had help and leave it at that."

Thomas wanted more but he could sense this was not the time to ask a lot of questions.

•   •   •

Damian was angry. "Damn it!" he said. "What the hell happened here!"

Damian was beside himself with frustration as he watched the plane fly out of range of their guns. He could see the plane was struggling to gain altitude but they were too far away to do anything. He had a headache that wouldn't quit and he let his source of information get away. He was looking for someone to blame. He was also afraid of the Vasquez family, the house guards knew too much already. They knew he brought two women to the family retreat without permission. That would not sit well with the Vasquez family or Santos.

Caleb wasn't doing much better except he had the added burden of Damian's anger. "Damian, we hit the plane, they won't get out of Colombian airspace."

"Shut up Caleb! I have to think."

The English speaking guard turned to Damian. "Señior Damian, shall I call the Vasquez family and notify them of this problem? They will have a solution and they know important people at the country's airports that can spot them for us. They can't get very far if the plane is damaged."

Damian heard his words but could not bring himself to leave his destiny to the Vasquez family. He was tired of them being in control. He was tired of being afraid of them and what they would do to him if he screwed up. He made a lot of money for them and himself, they had no idea how much he skimmed off the top. He could quit now and disappear. "That's it," he thought, "time to disappear."

"Caleb, drive us over to where the helicopter blew up."

When they arrived at the location of the explosion, Damian ordered everyone out of their cars.

"I want to see if that man is dead and if there is any information we can salvage from the fire."

To Caleb this was a strange request, but no one hesitated to get out.

Damian instructed the guards to go over to the chopper and see if they could find anything of value or clues indicating who the two men were that came in on it. When they approached Roberto's body one of them shouted to Damian—"His identification says he is DEA!"

As two of the guards walked over to the burned out chopper and another guard was rummaging through Roberto's dead body, Damian pulled his Uzi up from his side and sprayed them with bullets. None of the men had a chance to react or to defend themselves. They fell where they stood, each riddled with enough bullets to ensure their deaths. It would look like a gunfight as if the agents killed them. Damian was pleased with his planning and forward thinking.

Caleb stood by the H2 stunned. "Damian, are you crazy!?"

"No not crazy, just insurance to make things look right for us. This way I can tell the family, if we ever run into them, that they were killed in a gun battle with the DEA and others and that I shot the agent after he shot the guards. The explosion was part of the battle."

Caleb was afraid he was next. "What are you going to do now?" he asked with a slight tremor to his voice.

"We are going to drive out of here and head for the Medellin airport, get two tickets to the south of France and get lost for a while until things cool down."

"Am I going with you?" Caleb said about to wet his shorts.

"Yes, I need you to corroborate my story if anyone ever catches up to us." Damian dropped the Uzi next to Roberto's body, got in the Hummer with Caleb driving and drove away.

•   •   •

"We are losing altitude, buckle up everyone!" William was shouting instructions from the cockpit as Frank was trying to control the plane.

"Hey, what's going on?" came Jan's groggy voice.

Kellie went over to Jan and picked up her hand. "Hi baby, welcome back. How do you feel?"

"Like someone hit me in the head with a sledge hammer. What happened, one minute I am running through the woods, the next I'm on a plane?"

"It's a long story but suffice it to say we are safe from Damian for now. We are having a little plane trouble so I need you to rest your head. I love you, just hang in there. Marisa is right next to you."

"Marisa," Jan said. "Thank God you are alive." With that Jan laid her head on Marisa's shoulder and fell unconscious again.

"Don't worry Kellie, I've got her."

Marisa would do whatever it took to be sure nothing happened to Jan. After all she had saved Marisa from certain death more than once. The future for them all was uncertain but no matter what happened to her she was forever grateful for Jan's support as a lawyer and friend. She did not want to get Jan in trouble for helping her. She was determined to tell the government everything and that Jan had nothing to do with what happened.

Frank was desperately looking for a place to land. He wanted to land in Turbo but Frank seemed upset about that option. He was already over the Turbo airport talking to the tower.

"I can try for Turbo—it is very close."

"No Frank," William told him. "We can't go back there. Kellie and I had some significant problems there."

"It is the closest and we are running out of time," Frank replied.

"I told you to find something else; otherwise, I would rather land in the jungle. Apartado is not far from Turbo; we can make it." William insisted.

"Okay, okay, I can try," he told William through the headphones.

The ride was getting rougher and Frank was having trouble keeping the plane steady at the low altitude he was forced to fly. It was just a few more miles to the Apartado airstrip. Frank pushed the plane forward with the one engine on full throttle.

"There!" cried William pointing to the airstrip.

"I see it," replied Frank. "Tell everyone to buckle up; this is going to be a rough landing."

•   •   •

Damian decided to drive back to the house and get his things together before heading out. As he and Caleb drove up the driveway they could see several new vehicles parked outside. He recognized one of them; it was Santos. He stopped the H2 short and began to turn around.

"Caleb?" Damian said, "We need to get out of here now."

Caleb did not want to say anything, he was already afraid of Damian. He knew he would be killed if the Vasquez family saw them.

Caleb turned the Hummer around and left the area forever. Santos heard a vehicle and caught a glimpse of the H2 as it pulled away.

Damian and Caleb headed for Medellin to catch flights that would get them to the south of France.

•   •   •

"William, this is not going to be good. I am sorry if I kill you and your sister."

"Frank," William said, "right now I trust you and you can land this plane."

"Get in the crash position!" shouted William to everyone in the back.

Everyone took the required position with heads between their legs. Marisa helped bend Jan's head down between her knees and held the makeshift bandage against her head.

"What if we dump most of our remaining fuel to lighten the plane and help avoid possible fire?" suggested William.

"Okay," replied Frank, "good idea, I should have thought of that. There is not much left anyway since one of the bullets pierced the fuel tank on the left side."

Frank proceeded to dump the remaining fuel in both engine tanks but left enough for landing. As the ground got closer, Frank began to sweat, he had no idea where to set down the plane. In the back, Marisa was praying; Kellie was holding on, her heart racing, and Thomas was praying. .

" God, I have a family I want to see them again, please help Frank land this palne safely" Thomas prayed out loud.

"Marisa hold on to Jan, how is she doing?" Kellie asked.

"She is in and out. Better for her she doesn't know what is going on."

Kellie was worried not just for their lives but for what could happen if they landed in another unknown area of Colombia. Apartado was not far from Turbo and it was just as rough and rugged.

•   •   •

Santos was talking with Carlos Vasquez Jr., the oldest son of Manuel Vasquez. As they surveyed the damages to their house and spoke with the remaining guards who stayed behind, they learned of Damian's behavior and what he had done. As far as Carlos was concerned Damian's conduct was against the family protocol for low profiling of their operations. Damian had breached every procedure for taking care of problems but also in avoiding them. He had to be contained. As far as Santos was concerned that meant eliminating him.

Santos advised Carlos of what happened in Turbo when some of the locals loyal to the family had found out about Kellie's and William's inquiries. He did not know what or how Damian got into the country without notifying them. He knew that any visit would require notice to the family in case they wanted to meet to discuss business in the United States..

"Señior Vasquez, we need to sweep this house clean and remove any drugs and money in case the local police raid the compound as a show of force for the Americans who have demanded stepped up security and control of drug trafficking. Damian's actions here may bring the Federales to our doorstep."

"I agree Santos," Carlos replied. "Get the men to begin the process of clearing this house. We need to clear all the villas in this area just in case. They hold a lot of cash and drugs. Be sure to take away all the sodium pentothal for now. We will deal with cooperators later once we assess the damages Damian has caused us. Now go and find Damian and bring him back. I don't care if he is dead or alive."

• • •

As Frank looked below him he could see the Apartado landing strip. It would not be a smooth landing if they did not make the airport landing strip. All he could do was glide the plane in, reduce power at the last minute pull up and hope they survived.

"Heads down everyone!" William shouted.

"William, the minute we hit, pull the throttle back hard!" Frank instructed.

"Ok, Frank you can do this."

Slowly they began their descent. Frank was having trouble keeping the plane stable with just the one engine. The bullet holes and damage affected the wing stability and flaps. He was pulling with all his strength on the yoke.

"Hey!" Frank yelled back from the cockpit, "I'm getting some lift from the air below. It is swirling off the mountains creating an updraft. I might be able to keep us up a bit longer, maybe just enough to get us to the actual runway. It is just another mile. ."

Kellie was concerned that word had spread throughout the region of what went down in Turbo. She had visited Apartado for possible factory locations as well, and it too was a drug-supported town.

"Frank, we have to land somewhere else!" Kellie yelled.

"Well, little miss, would you rather crash and burn, or risk getting shot landing on some Colombian drug dealer's personal runway, or take our chances with a real runway and airport!" Frank was shouting to Kellie as he struggled to keep the plane from crashing.

"Look," Thomas said, "I think I can get us past the heat at the airport. I know some of these guys and can tell them you are in my custody and I need to get you to my police station in Medellin. I will cover for us, just get this plane on a real runway."

Gradually the plane descended . Frank was having trouble keeping the plane steady. He was having trouble controlling the landing.

"We are going to hit hard!" Frank shouted.

The plane landed on the concrete tarmac, skipped up, came back down, the front landing wheel collapsing. The nose was grinding and sparking.

"Pull hard, William!" Frank was slamming on the brakes, all flaps up but the flaps on the left wing would not respond. He was almost standing on the brakes while Frank pulled back hard on the yoke.

Just before the plane came to a stop it curved to the right. Frank had no control where the plane went.

"Hang on everyone; we are going to hit a fence!" cried Frank.

"What is after the fence!" screamed Kellie.

"The highway three hundred feet below the runway!" Frank yelled. His voice was clearly strained.

"God help us!" screamed Marisa.

Frank started screaming, "We are going to die, either we go over the fence onto the highway and burst into flames or the sparks will ignite the plane. I can't stop us. Everyone keep your heads down in the crash position!"

Suddenly the plane jerked violently and the left wing broke off the plane. The plane slid hard into the fence at the end of the runway. The fence broke but slowed the plane to a stop, but not before the front of the plane was teetering over the side to the highway below. It took a few seconds for everyone to realize what had happened.

"Ahhhhh!" screamed William. "We made it! Look! The fence stopped us just a few inches from dropping off the highway!"

Kellie got up and looked out the window. "Everyone off the plane now!"

"What's wrong Kellie?" asked Marisa.

"We are about to drop down to the busy highway below. The fence is barely holding the plane back."

"Get up now!" screamed Kellie.

As she said this the plane moved forward. That was enough to get everyone out of their seat belts and running for the front exit.

Kellie grabbed Jan's arm, Marisa on the other side. "Go!" cried Kellie, "Go now!"

Everyone was out of the airplane except William and Frank. Marisa started back up the stairs but Kellie sat Jan down on the tarmac and grabbed Marisa's arm to stop her. "No Marisa you can't go back in!"

"Let go of me Kellie, I need to get William out!"

Just as Marisa was pulling away from Kellie, William appeared at the top of the stairs of the exit. As he began his descent the plane started to move downhill.

"Jump William!" cried Marisa and Kellie at the same time. "Jump!"

William jumped from the top stair at the same time the plane broke through the fence that was holding it back and plunged to the highway below. Frank never left the pilot's seat before the plane landed and was hit by several cars, bursting into flames.

The explosion caused everyone to drop to the tarmac debris flying all around them. Kellie ran to cover Jan from the debris.

"Is everyone okay?" Kellie yelled over the noise.

"Yes!" cried Marisa.

"I'm okay!" yelled Thomas.

William was not answering. Kellie was helping Jan when Marisa started screaming. "Oh my God William, William are you okay? please answer me!"

William was lying on the ground and not moving.

"William! Please don't die on me! I just found you!" Marisa was holding Williams' head in her lap on the ground.

Slowly William started to move and open his eyes. "Hey sis." "

Marisa started to cry. "You were knocked unconscious from the explosion. Your leg is bleeding."

"I think I'm okay. Looks like some debris hit my leg. That's three wounds too many for me, I am done with guns, helicopters, and planes."

"Can you stand and walk, William?" asked Kellie.

"Yes I think so. Let's get out of here."

As they began to walk towards the terminal they realized sirens were headed their way.

"Crap, this is not good," Kellie said.

"Kellie, I am not doing well, I feel like I am going to throw up," Jan muttered. "I need to sit down."

"Baby, sit down on the tarmac. I'm pretty sure you have a concussion from being hit by a bullet. I am just glad the bullet grazed you and did not kill you."

Jan sat down and put her head between her knees. She was exhausted and she had a splitting headache.

As the sirens approached Thomas said, "Let me deal with this."

Kellie was not sure, but they were all too tired and worn down to fight back.

The airport fire detail arrived with the police and an ambulance. The fire-fighters were overwhelmed and had limited water resources but started spraying the flames from above the highway.. You could hear the sirens on the highway below arriving on the scene working to put out the fire and help those injured or dead.

The first officer to stop started speaking in Spanish to Thomas.

"William, what are they saying?" asked Kellie.

"Sounds like Thomas is trying to get medical help for me and Jan. The officer is asking how everyone got here to Apartado, what were we doing and about Jan's injuries. Thomas told them my injuries and Jan's were from the crash. Thomas is telling them that we are his prisoners," replied William with concern in his voice.

William continued to translate. "The officer offered his handcuffs to help and wanted to know why we were not cuffed already. Thomas said he had to release everyone before the crash to avoid anyone getting hurt."

Thomas and the officer approached Jan first. "Put your hands behind your back, miss," said Thomas in an unfamiliar tone.

Kellie jumped in between the officer, Thomas and Jan. "She is injured— you are not going to cuff her!"

The officer was about to physically intervene by grabbing Kellie when Thomas put his hand up and said in Spanish: "Por favor, no nessecito." The officer stopped.

"I am not going to let them cuff Jan!" Kellie declared.

Thomas put his hand up to stop everyone from arguing. "Kellie, stop I will handle this, you have to trust me."

Thomas began again speaking to the officer in Spanish who was now joined by several other officers and military personnel.

William translated what was being said. "They want to help Thomas transport us all to the local jail. Thomas is trying to tell them that he has the situation under control and that his prisoners are being cooperative. He is also saying that some of us are not prisoners but people helping him with a case he is working on. They want to know what the case is about, but Thomas is telling them it is of national security between the United States and Colombia."

Finally, Thomas got the officers to back off. "Listen," Thomas said to Kellie, "I need someone to be cooperative and act like my prisoners. I need to handcuff at least two of you."

"Fine," Kellie said, "William and Marisa are the real offenders here, so cuff them!"

"No!" cried Marisa, "William is hurt; he needs a doctor."

"Look we either do this my way," said Thomas, "or we get an escort from the local police and everyone gets cuffed including Jan."

"Ok" said William, "just be gentle."

"No!" Marisa insisted.

William tried to assure Marisa. "Marisa, it is going to be okay, let Thomas do what he must to get us out of here. Jan and Kellie have done nothing wrong but we have."

"Thomas is right Marisa," Kellie interjected, "We need to get out of her alive and not end up in a local jail."

Marisa relented and Thomas cuffed them both with the assistance of the local authorities. Thomas thanked the officers for the borrowed cuffs and promised to return them when he delivered his prisoners to the Federal authorities. The officers were still reluctant to let then go but eventually agreed to do so only if they drove them to their destination.

All of them got into two Jeeps and were taken to the terminal where they were escorted to two taxis who were instructed by the officers to take them to a local hospital for treatment and then to the courthouse where a local jail would hold the two prisoners until they could arrange for transportation to Medellin and then out of Colombia. The officers followed the taxis in one of the Jeeps to the hospital.

When they got to the hospital, Thomas spoke to the officers and asked if there was something he could do to let them get back to work. The answer was always the same, money.

Thomas said nothing but put his hand out with several hundreds in it. The officers first looked reluctant to take the money, but eventually took it all. They were not happy and were uncertain as to why a DEA agent would offer them a bribe to look the other way; nonetheless, they left Thomas alone with his so-called prisoners with a warning in clear Spanish that Thomas understood: Leave the area quickly. I If we see you tomorrow you will be arrested along with your friends. Thomas knew they saw through his feeble attempt to hide what might really be going on.

Thomas returned to his companions and took the cuffs off of Marisa and William. They entered the hospital in Apartado, Colombia. It was a small hospital, and not very sanitary looking, but there were nurses and doctors waiting to assist them.

The hospital treated William who required several stitches in his leg and re-bandaged his gunshot wound. Kellie told the doctor all his wounds came from the crash though it was clear they suspected something else had happened but asked no questions. William's burns were starting to heal and the doctor knew it so neither she or William commented on those injuries.

Jan was able to get bandaged up but needed some heavy medication to offset the headache pain caused by her injury. The wound required a couple of butterfly stitches but was not life-threatening. They were now on their own in trying to get out of Colombia. Kellie found a local coffee shop with internet access and a computer she could use for a fee. It did not take long to arrange flights back to the U.S. through Medellin. They all looked a little ragged and worn out having not had a shower or clean clothes in the past thirty six hours, but they were on their way back to the States. They were able to pass airport security in Medellin with Thomas flashing his credentials alerting the agents that he was transporting a potential cooperating prisoner back to the States. The airport agents demanded they fly back to the States with Marisa handcuffed so Thomas agreed and cuffed her hands in front. Kellie and William had their own passports, though William's was a fake, so they got through security with a few questions and a body search but nothing more.

"This is so uncomfortable, riding in a plane with handcuffs on," Marisa complained.

"I know," said Thomas, "but without them we would likely not be able to leave Colombia."

"Marisa, we will be okay," William added. "Just try and sleep, we are going to need all of our energy when we get back to figure out what to do."

They arrived in Atlanta five days after Marisa had escaped from federal prison. The customs agents wanted to know why no one had any bags. The agent called her supervisor who inquired of Thomas even further. He had to reveal some of the story but persuaded the supervisor to let them through to finish their legal business and turn Marisa in. The supervisor was concerned about the injuries to Jan and William.

"Agent Thomas, I'm not sure I can let these people go with you. First your story sounds a bit farfetched but second there are a lot of injuries here which you have told me came from a crash in Apartado, Colombia, a known drug area."

Jan was feeling much better after being able to relax and sleep on the plane flight home. "William and I were in a plane accident and were injured." She offered. "Agent Thomas is telling you the truth. I want nothing more than to go home, heal and get some rest. All our luggage was lost in the crash as well."

"But why are you with this prisoner and the agent in the first place?" the customs agent inquired further.

"I am an attorney and this lady is my client as is this gentleman" pointing to William but not offering him up as a possible criminal. We have been co-operating with the U.S. authorities and Colombia in a large undercover drug cartel investigation. These two have a lot of information and need to be on their way with Agent Thomas to New York to meet with the United States Attorney there."

"Well," the customs agent said, "it looks like there is a fugitive warrant for one of your group, a person named Marisa Herrera-Cardosas. We need to detain her."

"No you do not!' Thomas piped in with authority. "I have jurisdiction here and have arrested her. I am on my way to turn her in. I have no intentions of doing anything else, and you cannot stop me."

With some hesitancy the customs supervisor let them go with a warning.

"Okay, you can get on your way but if I find out you all are involved in something more sinister we will arrest everyone including you Agent Thomas."

None of what Jan and Thomas were telling the customs supervisor was far from the truth. No matter what Marisa had to turn herself in.

"What will you do now, Thomas?" asked Kellie.

"Well, I have to take Marisa and William in despite our experience together. I actually like them and see they want to do the right thing but I will have to go to Washington and file some kind of report and turn them in to the New York Marshals office. I really need to do this myself." Thomas replied, "I just can't let you take two heavy-duty drug dealers and help them disappear again, now can I?"

"No," Jan piped in. "But I have a deal for you if you will listen."

"Okay, I'm listening."

"I take them to my house in Atlanta for the weekend." Jan offered, "I just need a couple of days to sort out options with the Assistant United States Attorney in New York. I need some time to work out a deal."

Thomas hesitated. He was tired and knew the paperwork on this mess would be overwhelming. He already had to address what happened to Roberto and would need time to put everything together.

"Okay, here is what I can do. I will give you until Tuesday, but I want to meet you in New York to turn them in as my prisoners. This way my report will be mostly true and I will have fulfilled my duty as a federal agent. I will tell them I captured them in Colombia but will also tell them what happened. The DEA will want to know what happened to Roberto. I have to tell them the truth, a gun battle with a major drug cartel."

"I will need more time," replied Jan.

"No Jan, this is all I can do; take it or leave it. I have to trust you will surrender them at all. I am taking a huge risk not taking them in now. No one really knows where we are or what happened yet but if I failed to turn over a prisoner I could lose my job."

"Well I am not about to go to jail or risk my career, or for that matter yours, over this. Done, I will take what I can get. I will surrender them on Tuesday. I will meet you at the Federal Courthouse at the Marshals lockup in

New York at 3 p.m.."

•   •   •

The first thing Jan did when they all got to Jan and Kellie's place was call David.

On the other end of the phone Jan could hear David scream which set off heavy barking from Ranger.

"David, it is okay. Come over to our house and we will catch you up on events. Bring my baby with you."

Jan turned to Kellie and assured her Ranger was okay and they were both on their way to the house. "I could tell David was opening the door to his car before we were off the phone."

David did not live far from Jan and Kellie so he was there within ten minutes. He came in the house without knocking and Ranger came bounding in at his side. When Ranger saw Kellie and Jan he was beside himself yelping with great joy and wagging his whole body. Kellie and Jan got on their knees and hugged him. "Such a good dog Ranger, you took care of us and David as well. We missed you."

When Ranger saw Marisa and William he took a more serious stand and started barking until Kellie reassured him that they were friends. It took a minute, but soon he was getting pets from them both.

"Hey, what about me?" cried David.

Both Jan and Kellie realized that he was probably the person most affected by this ordeal. "David, we are so sorry you had to go through all of this," Jan said.

Through tears and hugs David had few words to offer other than, "I have never been happier to see you two in my life."

Kellie got a bottle of wine out and poured everyone a drink while they all went over the events of the last week with David. Ranger never left Jan and Kellie's side. If one left the couch he would pace back and forth between them until the one that left returned.

•   •   •

William and Marisa spent the night with Jan and Kellie in their two spare bedrooms while David took the couch. He was not interested in going home; he wanted to be near his chosen family. Ranger slept on Kellie and Jan's bed as usual. Everything was back to normal, at least from Ranger's perspective.

Monday came fast. Jan felt much better, as did William. Everyone went to Jan's office to call Assistant United States Attorney Jake Harden in New York.

"Jan, are you all right? David told me what was going on.."

"Jake, listen, I have a deal to make with you for both Marisa and William, interested?"

"I will always listen to reason but they both are fugitives."

"I know but let me tell you what happened."

Jan put the phone on speaker and she and Kellie told their harrowing story deliberately leaving out where Marisa and William were. Marisa and William were instructed to stay silent lest Jan and Kellie be charged with harboring two fugitives from the law. When Jan and Kellie finished there was silence on the phone.

"This sure is an incredible story, Jan," Jake finally said. "I know you, and I know Kellie from her FBI days so it is hard not to take you seriously, but you have got to know this is a tough one to believe. Where are my two fugitives?"

"Well," Jan started, "that's where things get interesting. Marisa and William have advised me they want to turn themselves in but have asked me to try and resolve both their cases before doing so. How about I bring them to the U.S. Marshals office in New York for voluntary surrender and full cooperation? In return, Marisa gets five years in prison, no escape charges added to her indictment, credit for time served and William is not charged but fully cooperates."

"Jan, that does not sound like a good deal for me since we have not only a major drug dealer to prosecute but one that escaped from a federal prison with the help of her brother. We also found a dead prison guard who worked on Marisa's floor when the escape was executed."

Jan looked at Marisa, puzzled over this revelation. Marisa shook her head "no," to having any information about a dead prison guard.

"Jake, you have no proof Marisa had anything to do with the prison guard or that her brother helped her. In fact we can give you the man who did help her and then kidnapped both of us and tried to kill Marias and me. He is probably responsible for the guard's death as well."

"If Marisa comes in, she has to tell us everything including what her brother's involvement is with the drug trade and the escape. I will talk to my supervisor on a deal but my offer is six years on the drug case with credit for time served and an additional eighteen months on the escape. The brother serves three years if I like what he has to offer as well. Take it or leave it. If they had nothing to do with the prison guards death I might be able to sell the deal to my superiors."

"I think I can get Marisa to agree to this and you will get the whole story of Marisa and her brother's lives and how it became entwined with Damian Garrison who is David Stone who is probably a number of people all wrapped up in one. We can help you set up a sting to capture him and I suspect he will sing like a bird on the drug family he works for. If you give us this deal, you will set in motion the collapse of a major drug cartel in Colombia and the United States. When the whole cartel collapses, we want the option of more time off. Interested now?"

It took Jake a few minutes to decide but he was interested. "Ok Jan, I will take this to my bosses and get back with you today."

"Thanks Jake, it is a good deal for everyone." With that Jan hung up the phone and told Marisa and William that she thought everything would work out.

Marisa did not want either of them to serve any time, but after all she did commit some serious crimes and people died. Looking back on what had happened, she was just happy that she and her brother were still alive.

Jake's call came in that same afternoon with a confirmation his deal was accepted by his bosses if the cooperation proved of significant value. On Tuesday, Jan met Thomas and they both escorted Marisa and William to federal Marshals office in New York as promised and turned them in.

•   •   •

It had been several weeks since they left Colombia. Damian and Caleb were walking the beach at Saint Tropez in the south of France drinking beer. They did not see her at first; she was wearing a long black and white flowing tunic with black capri leggings and white sandles. She now had short hair again but looked so much different with a tan.

"Well Alan," Caleb started, "we made it out alive and thanks for bringing me along. This is the life."

"I have told you not to call me by my real name. Use my new fake name Evan Jones. I need to keep all my old names under rap including my real birth name! Got it?"

"Yeah, I got it. It's hard to keep up with all your fake names but I got it!" Caleb replied.

As they continued to walk Damian looked up in the distance at the figure coming towards them. There were a lot of people on the beach but none wearing what Marisa had on. Damian kept looking, not sure what he was seeing.

"Caleb, do you see that girl there with the short dark hair and black and white tunic?"

"Where?" Caleb asked.

"There, about fifty yards ahead of us, see her?" Damian pointed to Marisa.

"Shit Alan, , I mean Evan, that can't be her. How would she get here?'

"I don't know but she looks great."

"What are you going to do?" Caleb asked.

"Wave at her. If that is her, she must still love me so I can use that to get her back and then deal with her the way I should have."

"Alan, or Evan or whatever, , think about it, why would she trust you after you tried to kill her twice. I don't like this."

"You have a point Caleb. But she is in a foreign country; so what can she do to me here?"

Just as Damian was about to wave at what he believed was Marisa he saw her hand slightly move and point towards him. He lifted his hand to wave when suddenly he was hit from behind and lay flat on the sand. He turned his head to see Caleb down there with him.

"What the hell is going on here!" Damian cried.

"DEA, dirtbag, you are under arrest for possession and sales of illegal narcotics for the purpose of importing and distributing them into the United States."

Then in perfect English with a French accent came another voice. "Yes and we are the French police arresting you on behalf of the United States of America and in cooperation with their government. Welcome to France, dirtbag!"

Damian was stunned at what he was hearing. "You can't arrest me for conspiracy in France, they don't recognize that crime."

"Right Damian, or rather Alan Johnson, we are not arresting you for conspiracy."

"Who are you telling me all this and how did you find me?" As soon as Damian said this he knew, it had to be Marisa. He knew he should never have let her get close to him and travel with him to his favorite hideouts.

"Get up, both of you." Thomas was facing Damian a smile of complete satisfaction on his face. "Let's go."

Damian looked back to see Marisa but she was gone. Damian knew what he was about to do next, he had a boat load of cooperation information to give the feds for his benefit. He had been smart enough to keep records, names, places, murders and details of who did what and where. He knew the corrupt DEA and Custom agents and he would be walking free in a few years.

As Damian walked away in handcuffs, he never heard the shot fired from three hundred yards away. Damian fell in an instant, a clean shot to his head.

The agents and police saw Damian fall and hit the ground. They did not hear the shot but saw the gaping wound immediately and recognized it as a gunshot. They all hit the ground, guns drawn in case of a second shot. They could not see where the gunfire came from. They could, however, hear Caleb crying and begging to be placed in witness protection.

"Help me, you got to put me in witness protection; they are going to kill me too."

"Why should we care about you Caleb?" Thomas asked as he jumped up weapon drawn looking for someone with a high powered rifle.

"Because I know what Damian, rather Alan, knew and I know where the drugs come from and how they get in the U.S. and where he hides his information, information that will tell you everything you need to know about his operation and the Vasquez family." Caleb was running his mouth as fast as he could to get protection from being killed by the Vasquez family. He knew who shot Damian, he knew too much.

"Well Caleb," Thomas mused, "we will think about it and see what you have to offer."

Thomas and some of the local police rushed to their vehicles while others began to scour the area trying to find the shooter. Others remained with Damian's body until a local medical examiner and coroner could arrive. They would never find Santos as he walked calmly down the street carrying a rolling luggage bag looking like any other tourist.

Special thanks goes out to Attorney Elizabeth Brandenburg who read the book, liked it and gave great editing advice. Also to Sara Snider who provided additional support, positive editing advice and direction. Finally, Dorrance publishing services and staff who provided their full support in bringing this book to life.